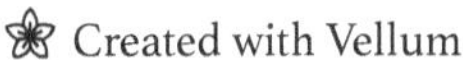 Created with Vellum

BIG GAME

C.K. WILES

HOT CHOCOLATE PRESS

G rumpy's Happy Shack. My favorite little dive bar had it all. The tile floors were worn so thin they seemed to disappear in places, and every table had different chairs, creating a more shabby than chic look. The one attempt at ambiance came from the cheap icicle lights hanging above rows of multicolored bottles. Countless elbows, spilt beers, and deliberated dreams had dulled character into the bar top which held secrets of its own. If the happiest place on Earth meant screaming children, hot asphalt, and overpriced rodent paraphernalia, I would take Grumpy's any day.

"Hey, Denise. Where's Rob?"

I looked up. It was Grumpy himself, Al Smith. All the regulars had a running pool on whether or not Smith was his real name. Al looked like he had spent his life fighting off rebel guerrillas and man-eating anacondas in the deepest jungles of South America. Not sure what brought him to our quaint town at the base of the Rockies, but I'm glad he's here and has given us locals a place to hang out.

"He'll be here any minute." I smiled. "Can I get a rum and Coke while I'm waiting?"

Al returned my smile with a scowl.

"It's not like you are that busy." I scanned the room to see a smattering of people scattered here and there. "You know you love me."

He grunted back at me and went behind the bar to prepare my drink.

"Denise," a slurred voice called from across the room.

I groaned inwardly and glanced toward the door, wishing Rob would hurry up.

"Denise, you look great tonight. What have you been up to?"

Terry "Two Step" Briley was Golden's resident irritation. He hit on anything with a pulse and rarely had the money to pay for his own drinks, but he still managed to remain so inebriated he couldn't take more than two steps without stumbling.

"What can I do for you, Terry?" I made the mistake of glancing up, and Terry shot me a conspiratorial wink. It was enough to make me yank my eyes away in revulsion.

"Do for me? Nothing. I mean, I just wanted to say hello. See how you're doing and all. Your boyfriend coming in? Did he give you a free pass tonight?"

"He's not my boyfriend, and yes, Rob will be here any second. So, if you don't mind ..."

Terry shuffled back a step and put his hands up. "Okay, I can take a hint. No need to get testy."

When he turned to walk away, Terry bounced off something. I looked back to see what it was. Al had blocked his path like a granite rockslide, and he wore a scowl that would curdle milk. Terry backed off him so fast he almost ran into me again.

"How about you stake your claim over there, champ?" Al jabbed a thumb over his shoulder. "If I have to come back to deliver something other than coffee, your head will deliver your own prostate exam."

Terry didn't say another word. He just offered a sort of half smile then did his stiff man drunk walk over to the other end of the bar.

"Thanks, Al. I don't know why you put up with that guy."

"Ambiance." Al set my glass down on the table. "Anything else?"

"Don't I get one of those fancy little napkins to put under my drink?"

Al stared at me for a moment, wearing a scowled mask of disdain, then he turned around and walked back to the bar.

I laughed. Gotta love Al.

"Hey." Now that was a familiar voice that always made me smile. "Sorry I'm late."

Rob waved as he made his way through patrons chatting at tables or loitering in the middle of the room. He almost always looked the same: dark green Forest Ranger pants, a semi-pressed khaki shirt displaying his badge, and a flat brimmed hat. He finished off his rugged look with an unshaven face and muddy boots. We were just friends, but if the there was ever a calendar for hot Park Rangers, he would be Mr. December.

He put his hand on my shoulder. "I would have been here sooner, but I had to wrap up a few things at work."

"Get caught up in a big fishing license sting?" I jabbed. "You're lucky to escape with your life."

"Ha, ha," Rob took off his hat and threw his coat over his chair across from me. "I do not write tickets for fishing licenses. Okay, hardly ever. The ISB does investigations for the National Park Service. Thus, the Investigative part in *Investigative Services Bureau*. Why are you always busting my chops?"

I took a sip of my drink. "Because it's fun."

Rob gave me the stink eye and walked over to the end of the bar. He grabbed a glass, filled it with ice, and reached over to fill it with soda water from the gun. He raised it to Al, who acknowledged the gesture with a dismissive flip of his bar towel.

"Al must be in a good mood," Rob said. "He has his yellow shirt on."

Al's work uniform consisted of desert combat boots, military fatigue cargo shorts, and a colorful half-unbuttoned Hawaiian shirt. You could always tell his mood by how bright the color was.

"Yeah," I said. "He even brought my drink and ran Terry off. Next thing you know, he'll be telling jokes."

"I heard that," Al shouted in our general direction without looking up.

Rob laughed and sat down across from me. "So, what's the occasion? You actually look, I don't know, relaxed."

He motioned to my hair, which I had done up in a long ponytail. I usually wore it down in long, brown ringlets to accentuate my blue eyes. In the corporate event planning business, it helped to have an edge, even if it was as superficial as attraction. This evening, however, I had even opted to do away with my jacket and show off my sleeveless blouse. Be still my intrepid heart.

"I closed out my two big accounts today, one here in town other in Denver, so I knocked off an hour early and headed here to relax a little before you arrived."

Rob stopped mid-sip and stared at me. After several seconds of frozen wonder, he lowered his glass to the table and squinted as he leaned forward. "Who are you, and what have you done with my friend?"

"Shut up." I glared at him.

"Seriously. I have a gun. I'll shoot you if I have to."

"You'll have to get your bullet out first, Barney. You sure you have permission for that?"

Rob winced. "Never mind. It's you again."

"I can relax, you know." I took another drink of my rum and Coke. "I do it all the time."

Rob let out a laugh. "No, you don't. Your idea of relaxing is working in the office after hours so no one bothers you."

I nodded. "That's relaxing."

"No, that's working in a relaxed atmosphere. Relaxing is where you go home, find a hobby, read a book, have a relationship ..."

"Well, I have you, don't I?" I leaned forward.

"I don't count. I'm more like a dysfunctional counselor. When was the last time you had a real relationship?"

"I don't need relationships, besides look who's talking. You're so buried in your Boy Scout routine that you barely have time to go home. At least working is a necessity for me. If I had your kind of nest egg, I would never work again."

Rob's gaze fell, and he stared into his glass.

"I'm sorry. I didn't mean it like that." I took hold of his hand. "You know I miss Susan too."

"It's fine. I know what you meant." He took a long drink of his soda.

I sighed and sat back in my chair. "Well, that was a real mood setter, huh?"

Rob looked up and offered me a crooked smile, then his eyes flitted up over my head and his smile disappeared. There was the screech of a table being bumped across the floor, and I knew Terry was headed back for round two.

"Denise said you're not her boyfriend. Why not? She not good enough for you? Denise is a nice girl," he slurred as he stood over Rob. "You should treat her better."

I glanced toward the bar, but Al had disappeared. Probably headed back into the storeroom and Terry figured this was his chance.

"Why don't you head back over to your table." Rob smiled. "I'll have Al bring you something when he gets back. We're just talking. There's no need for trouble."

Terry let out a long breath, flapping his lips like a horse. "There's no trouble as long as you treat Denise right. She's a lady."

Terry put his gross, sweaty hand on my shoulder, and Rob

stood, his chair scraping along the floor. The bar quieted, but Terry didn't seem to notice. He swayed then leaned down, half closing his eyes and puckering his lips. Fortunately, he lost his balance and wound up throwing all his weight against my shoulder rather than following through with his slobbering token of affection. If Rob hadn't have caught him, we would have both gone over in a heap.

"Hey, get off of me." Terry got his feet under him, closed one eye to focus on Rob, then threw a haymaker all the way from the Colorado state line. Rob ducked it with no problem, caught Terry's arm and twisted his wrist into some sort of ninja pretzel lock that had the inebriated Casanova standing on his toes, yelping in pain.

"I just wanted to say hi. I'll go back to my table. You said you would get me another drink."

"Sorry, friend." Rob steered Terry using his arm like the rudder on a ship. Together they headed toward the front where Al already held the door open.

Terry did little to resist.

Before Al let him exit, he held out a hand and scowled. "Where are they?"

"Aww, come on, not that."

Al just stood there glaring like he might gnaw Terry's nose off if he didn't give him an answer.

"Fine," he finally relented. "Front pocket."

Al patted him down then reached into his right pocket and fished out his car keys. "Sit on the bench out front until you sober up." He handed Terry his coat. "If you move, I'll send Rob out to pull your fingers off."

Terry tried to look back, but Rob must have applied a little pressure, and Terry moved forward again. As soon as he was out the door, Rob let go. Al slammed the door shut, and Rob turned around to a smattering of applause.

His eyes darted around the room as if he just realized there were other people in the bar. He offered a weak smile by way of response before returning to our table. I knew what he was going to say before he got there.

He grabbed his jacket and shoved an arm in the sleeve, opening his mouth to offer some sort of apology.

I held up a hand to stop him. "Don't worry about it, Boy Scout. You are an insufferable good guy. You know that?" I got up and gave him a quick kiss on the cheek. "Thanks for saving me."

He smiled as he put his hat on. "Yeah, you could've taken him."

"But I didn't have to." I winked at him.

"I can give you a lift home too."

"In your Jeep with Terry? I'm not sure whether his compliments or his breath would kill me first. No thanks."

"I'm pretty sure he'll be too busy barfing out the window to admire your eyes."

I laughed. "I'll be fine. I'm going to have another drink then head home myself. I'll call for a Lyft if I need to."

Rob nodded. "Good idea. Talk care of yourself. Same time tomorrow?"

"As always," I said.

Rob walked out the door. I shook my head. Boy Scout through and through. I let my eyes play across the room. The place wasn't packed. A few couples, a few tables full of guys watching the Monday night football game, then I found him. A lone soul, sitting at the end of the bar, watching the small screen mounted in the corner. Good looking, pressed shirt, nice haircut, and his shoes looked like Italian leather. I downed my drink and got up, taking my blazer with me. Time to see what this lonely stranger was doing at Grumpy's Happy Shack.

CHAPTER TWO

I should have stayed with Denise at the bar. I let out an exasperated breath before I threw off the covers, turned on the lamp, and sat on the edge of the bed, resting my head in my hands. At least then I would have had some company. As it was, my house played host to more painful memories than I cared to count. An empty bed, photos of lost moments, and a closet full of clothes no one would wear again. Reminders of what I had lost lurked around every corner. At times they consumed me until I could hardly breathe.

My slippers beckoned me with their soft, dark lining, so I shoved my feet inside and shuffled off to my office. The light was on and the computer running. No point in shutting it down when sleep evaded me like a bobcat's ghost.

The springs on the old, wooden office chair creaked in protest as I sat down, sending empty echoes throughout the house. Susan had loved this chair. She had gotten it at a garage sale. Said it gave my office character. Every time I sat in it, the sound made me smile—and want to cry.

No new emails about the case. Not that I expected any at this hour. I had waited months to land something I could sink my teeth into. Now that the Forestry Department had assigned me something big, I wanted to be sure I didn't screw it up. I would be off and running as soon as I had their files and be happy for the distraction.

I clicked through a few more items, deleting junk mail—deleting more junk mail. Then I came to it. Another email from Susan's family. Why couldn't they just leave me alone? They had never liked me much. Thought she had married beneath her. Why would a wealthy, educated woman anchor herself to a Park Ranger? I asked myself that same question more than once. The answer had always been the same. It hadn't mattered. She chose me, and I chose her. We loved each other. We had been happy, and nothing could ever change that ... until something did.

I realized my jaw was clenched as tight as my fist, and I forced myself to relax before opening the email. It had all the same jargon. You have been summoned to appear ... funds are not at your disposal ... estate should be liquidated ... It all amounted to the same thing. Her family couldn't stand that I had anything that belonged to her, especially money. As far as they were concerned, I was living in their house, had control of their accounts, and drove their car. Well, maybe not that last part. I doubt any of them would stoop so low as to drive my old Jeep, even if Susan and I had purchased it together.

It wasn't even like her family needed the money. Not that I did either. They were rich beyond rich, and I could easily live on my salary. I just didn't want to give in to them. Not after the way they had treated her. Not after the way they had shut Susan out for marrying me. I would sooner burn every last dollar than see it go back to them. My lawyer said I had nothing to worry about. The money was mine. But it still riled me up every time they sent me something.

I deleted the email with a slam of the computer mouse and shut the computer down. The screen darkened, reflecting how I felt inside. I wondered, like always, what I should do. How was I supposed move on with this void in my chest? The chair beneath me squeaked, sending its call out among my hollow home, and I stood to walk over to the railing that overlooked the living room. A rustic sofa covered with blankets. Remnants of another battle with my nighttime demons. I had to get out. Had to find my own way. As much as it hurt, I needed to move out of this house, escape these memories, and find a way to make new ones.

Denise came to mind. She would understand. She had been Susan's best friend and now mine. We had relied on each other so much after Susan's death, that I wasn't sure I could have done it without her. She had always been there for me, and I for her.

It was time to let go of the house and everything in it. With the decision made, relief seeped through me, and I knew it was the right choice. I would talk to Denise tomorrow and ask for her help. Then I would find a way to keep Susan in my heart without losing my mind.

CHAPTER THREE

I awoke to a sharp pain akin to an icepick being lodged into the base of my skull. I swept my long hair off my face and glanced over at the clock. The numbers glowed an angry blue. Three in the morning. I had painstakingly built a jackhammer headache at Grumpy's, and it would take more than a couple of hours to tear it back down.

My head throbbed as I rolled over, drawing a groan out of my throat. I should have taken Rob up on his offer to drive me home while I had the chance. At least my memory hadn't taken a hike along with my senses. Handsome laid next to me, all curled up, mouth half open and snoring about as loud as an electric car. His hair still looked perfect, and I was pretty sure not a drop of drool had escaped his lips. If there was such a thing as sleep grooming gnomes, he had one.

I turned my face into my pillow and let out a little scream. I knew better than to bring a guy back to my apartment. Only two hours and I had to be up for work. I was stuck. It wasn't like I could sneak out and leave a nice note. There would be hell to pay for this one, I just knew it.

Handsome let out a sigh and smiled a little bit in his sleep. I rolled my eyes and reached out to smack him on the cheek in rapid succession until he woke up enough to dodge my mini assault.

"Good morning." I put on a smile and raised myself up on an elbow while I used my other hand to cover myself with the blankets. "Didn't mean to fall asleep on you like that."

Handsome smiled back at me and yawned. "That's all right. I figured we would grab some breakfast when we woke up. What time is it?"

I stifled a cringe. We were starting the dance already. "It's three. Look, I really have to get to work early so ..."

Handsome's smile faltered, transforming into something more like a lost puppy. "Oh, right. Guess I didn't think about that. Sorry."

He rolled out of bed and searched the floor next to him for his clothes. He found none. "Um, I think my stuff's still out there."

He pointed toward the living room where we had shed everything but our lustful needs.

I nodded. "Guess we got a little crazy on the way in."

Handsome shuffled off to the other room, and I watched him go. It was clear why I had been so attracted to him. Well built, boyish charm. If I were looking for a steady thing, he might fit the bill.

"Found 'em," he called from the other room. A moment later he came strolling in, buttoning his pants and carrying his shirt.

"Tonight was fun. I'd love to see you again."

More inward cringing. "I had fun too. Maybe we'll run into each other again sometime."

Awkward pause. Lots of staring, silence, and computing time on his part. Just when I thought he might get it, he broke down. "Well, can I get your number? Then I can call you later and maybe we can arrange another time to go out?"

I gave him a weak smile. "Look, I'm really busy with work and all. I had fun, but I'm not looking for anything serious."

"I'm not asking you to marry me." Handsome let out a laugh. "I just thought, you know, we could go out again and get to know each other a little better."

Oh, I knew. I knew all too well. Get to know each other turned into, "Why do you have to work so much, and why can't we spend more time together?" It was always the same. Amazing sex could never be just that. They always wanted more.

"Look, you don't want to know me better. I am no catch. Last night was fun. Let's just leave it at that."

Handsome stared at me for a minute, then pulled his shirt on. "Too bad. Maybe I'll stop by sometime and see if you've changed your mind." He winked.

And there was the reason I never brought guys back to my place. "I don't think so." I pulled myself up to a seated position and eyed him as he did his buttons. "If we run into each other, great. But like I said, I'm pretty busy. Work takes up most of my time, and I don't hang around home all that much. Plus, you don't want to get mixed up with someone like me."

"All right then." Handsome shrugged. "I guess I'll get going."

He turned to leave but then he paused and looked back at me. "For the record, I think you're a great catch. Dodge those lures for too long, and you may wind up believing that lie you tell everyone—including yourself. You're a beautiful person, Denise. I would count myself lucky to know you. Lots of people would."

Handsome headed out, and I heard him open the bolt on the front door. "By the way," he called out from the other room. "I'm leaving my card on your table. If you ever change your mind, look me up."

The door shut, and the room went silent, leaving me alone with one of the nicest things anyone had ever said to me. Hell to pay was right. Nothing stung more than sincerity.

CHAPTER FOUR

The trail appeared about twenty minutes into my zig-zagging hike through the dense, patchy, snow-covered forest. I automatically checked for my gun. The sun had pushed away most of the damp morning chill, but the fog still lingered in the trees. I knew most of my woods better than the streets of Golden, and this area was no exception. It paid to know what lurked in your own back yard. It made things that much harder for a stranger to slip in unnoticed.

Grateful for the growing warmth, I unzipped my coat a bit and appreciated that the snow had melted in some places. My foot falls were quiet on the damp needle beds. I took care to keep it that way. Denise could poke fun all she wanted, but in the end, out here in the middle of nowhere, rangers faced down armed, angry, and sometimes drunk or illegal hunters. It was a formula for disaster. One wrong move, and it would take weeks to find my body—if they found it at all.

I ran my hand over the bark of a tree. Three large holes had been drilled into the trunk. Someone had mounted a sturdy, high-end trail-camera to find out what sort of wildlife lived in the area. It was similar to what I had seen at the other locations. I was close.

A few more minutes, and I found it. Another sign of a trail-cam, but this time it was not scanning for wildlife. The people who had installed this one wanted a show.

I followed the direction it would have pointed and saw the tell-tale signs of a struggle. The thought of a poor animal trapped in an archaic snare infuriated me. It was clear they were after something big. The groundcover had been swept away, and the chain from the trap bolted to the tree still remained. The animal tracks led off into the woods, and I knew what I would find there too.

A fit of frustration and rage caused me to drive a fist into the tree trunk next to me. I was already too late. I always was. If I didn't find a way to get ahead of these people, they were going to do this again and again.

I hurried in the direction of the lamed animal anyway, hoping to be wrong. The blood trail in the snow made following the animal easy. By the looks of it, the poor creature had moved slowly, plodding along on three legs at best, flopping over to rest every few yards. It didn't stand a chance.

The crows guided me the rest of the way in from there. I heard them cawing over their new meal. When they gathered in numbers like this, they were called a murder rather than a flock. Aptly named in this case. When I came to the clearing, my heart dropped. I clenched my teeth in anger, watching dozens of birds bob and bounce over the thin layer of crimson stained snow. I shooed them off to examine the headless carrion splayed out in the middle—a huge, male gray wolf with a thick dazzling coat. He had been riddled with bullet holes.

"Damn it!" I yelled. These people weren't hunting. This was the sick annihilation of a living, breathing animal for nothing more than a souvenir. The fact that they targeted endangered predators made it that much worse. These scumbags had killed a beautiful animal and taken their prize—a head to mount on a trophy wall. The rest they left here to rot in the forest.

I glanced around the area, hoping to see something, anything that would help me catch these killers. Wolves weren't indigenous to the Colorado Rockies. That meant the hunters had found an incredibly rare specimen here—doubtful—or they had shipped one in. The latter was more likely, and it made sense. Hunting an endangered species on its native land would be problematic, to say the least. Bringing it to a place where hunting was common, and the species was not found in the wild, made it much easier. Especially when you lamed it, chained it to a tree, then set it free right before the hunting party arrived. The mere thought made me want to be sick.

My search turned up nothing I hadn't found before. One set of tracks leading straight in and then one set of tracks leading straight out again. Four people, likely male. Three wearing what looked like new boots, judging from their prints, and the fourth wearing boots that had seen more use. No doubt the guide.

These were pleasure expeditions for the sick and twisted. Hunting parties for people so rich they didn't have time to track, wait, or pursue. They just wanted to kill for the fun of it, not because they wanted food for their tables.

I shooed away the marauding cloak of black, feathered gluttons and bent down to cradle the majestic animal who had lived the last few days of his life in such misery. The least I could do was to dispose of the remains with a little dignity. Maybe I could even discover something by examining what was left. Anything was worth a shot. These butchers seemed determined to decimate several endangered populations, but I'd be damned if they'd do it in my own backyard.

CHAPTER FIVE

I slammed my breaks as a bright yellow VW Bug turned in front of me, unceremoniously ladling the entire contents of my venti, nonfat, vanilla latte onto my brand-new beige skirt.

I screeched both at the other driver, then at the hot liquid seeping through to my thighs. The finger I held up in the window did little good, as the driver of the yellow Bug sped away, leaving me to sit at the stoplight. I reached down to pull my steaming skirt away from my legs and grabbed a few napkins stashed in my console to dab up my liquid breakfast.

"I can't believe this." I growled to no one in particular. "A hippy cheerleader cuts me off, my skirt is ruined, I have no coffee, and my hangover is going for an Olympic world record. What else could possibly go wrong?"

The light turned green, and I managed to make it the rest of the way to the office without rear-ending any sorority queens. At least I'd have time to change. No one bothered to come in early on a Monday or any other day for that matter.

The second I rounded the front row of parking spots, I knew my morning was riding the rat express straight into the sewer. My spot, or at least the spot I always parked in, was taken. Sure, there were other spots. Pretty much all of them. But that was *my* spot, and it was occupied by a bright yellow VW Bug.

This could not be happening.

I careened into the spot next to the lemon-colored monstrosity, making sure there was less than six inches between my car and the Bug's driver's side door.

"Try and get in now, you quinoa-loving hippie freak."

My door slammed so hard the whole car shook, and I stomped into the office, satisfied to have evened at least part of the score—for now.

When the elevator doors opened on my floor, I found Jim, my boss and owner of Platinum Events Planning. He leaned against the wall, trying not to look like he was waiting for me to get off the elevator. What was with the whole world showing up to conspire against me today?

"Oh, hey, Denise. I'm glad I caught you. I hoped you might be in early today." He looked down at my skirt. "Did you spill something on your way in?"

"Some jerk cut me off in traffic, and wait, I'm early every day. You know that." I eyed his friendly smile with suspicion. "What's going on?"

"Come to my office. I want to give you some good news."

Jim turned and made his way toward his door.

"Can it wait just a sec? I want to go —"

"Come on," he interrupted without looking back. "This won't take long."

I sighed and followed him. Changing clothes would have to wait a few more minutes.

Jim held the door for me when I walked in, and I was surprised to see a stranger sitting across from his desk. A perky-looking red head all dolled up in a frilly, yellow blouse and matching yellow pumps.

My eyes narrowed as I realized this had to be my rolling ray of irritation.

"Denise, meet Kacey." He gestured toward her.

She stood up and reached out her hand. I glanced at it but did not respond in kind.

Jim continued. "I know how hard you work. Too hard in fact, and I want to expand our clientele. Kacey is going to be your new assis —"

"Please don't say assistant." I interrupted, holding up a hand to stop him and ignoring the pageant queen. "That's just another way of saying you hired someone to replace me, but you want me to train her first."

Kacey sunk back into her seat as if she were mired in quicksand.

Jim laughed. "Don't be ridiculous. This place would fall apart without you. Kacey is going to help manage your accounts, take some of the load off so you don't have to work so hard."

"But I like to work hard, Jim. That's what I do." I gave him a strained smile.

He seemed to realize Kacey still sat there, staring at the two of us as if she were watching a horror matinee and all the characters had just come to life around her.

"Maybe you could wait for us outside? Denise and I need to discuss a few things."

"Yes," I said. "While you're waiting, why don't you move your car out of *my* parking spot?"

Kacey stood up, gave us an uncomfortable smile, and walked out without saying a word.

The door closed behind her, and Jim's face turned to stone. "What is wrong with you? That's a very nice young lady, and you treated her like garbage. If I didn't know any better, I'd say you were scared."

I laughed. "Scared? Of her? Why? Because she is younger,

prettier, fresh out of college, and probably sleeps standing up so her face doesn't wrinkle?"

"Come on, Denise, calm down. Seven years ago, you were fresh out of college too. This will be a good thing for you. Kacey has fantastic credentials. Give her a chance. She won't disappoint you."

"Haven't I always come through for you? Don't I always get the job done? Even if you aren't looking to replace me, I don't need some debutant drooling over my shoulder, dying for me to screw up. I work alone. I always have. Give her to someone else. Let Trisha have her. I'll bet she would love an assistant."

"Trisha handles a quarter the load you do and doesn't work twelve-hour days just to keep up."

"I'll bet Kacey put in some overtime with you to land this job."

His eyes got big, and he stared at me.

I didn't know why I said things like that. Sometimes my bruised ego just took over my mouth and vomited the worst phrase imaginable for the situation. I never meant it, and it almost always did way more harm than good.

The silence between us grew so heavy a linebacker couldn't shove it out of the way.

"Kacey stays." His words came out through clenched teeth. "You will mentor her, and she will assist you with your accounts. I want to grow this company, and I can't do that watching you work yourself into an early grave. If that's unacceptable, then I guess you'll have to leave."

My mouth fell open, both in shock and to say ... I had no idea what to say. He had just told me to take Kacey or quit. To be fair, he also said he thought I was working myself to death, and he didn't want to see it happen. I knew he was right, at least on some level. I nodded and opened the door to Jim's office, knowing I should apologize for my comment but not quite able to do it. My ego was good at that trick too. Jim didn't say anything else as I left.

I headed for my cubicle, looking for my new assistant and a big pair of scissors. He had hired Kacey out of generosity and kindness, but all I saw was a threat. Gifts always came with strings attached, and this one had tangled yellow ribbons all over it. I would be ready to cut them the second they appeared.

CHAPTER SIX

Isaac Galindo was one of my best friends in the Ranger Service. He always had his nose to the ground and was on a first name basis with every mouse, rabbit, and owl living in the forest. If anyone could help me find these assholes, he could. On the other hand, if there was anyone who would be personally insulted by these poachings, it was him too.

"Oh, snap. Look who it is." Isaac stood from his desk and came to greet me at the door. "It's Mr. I.S.B. fancy pants himself. What are you doing down here? Get tired of the glamorous life and want to do some real work again?"

I snickered and shook his hand. "I figured I'd come see if you still sat at that desk all day, working on your waistline and surfing the wicked wilderness sites."

"You know it. A body like this doesn't come from a stuffy, old gym. I had to reach for it."

"Reach for the doughnuts, you mean."

Isaac laughed and pointed toward a white box perched on the break counter across the room. "That would hurt way more if it weren't true. You want one? I've got a bear claw with your name on it."

I held up a hand in protest. "I'm good. I actually came down to talk a little shop, if you don't mind. You know these woods better than anyone. I want to get your take on a case I'm working on."

Isaac held both hands to his chest. "I feel like I should curtsey or something."

"Come on, I'm serious." I shouldered past him and slumped into a chair next to his desk, a typical government issue piece of furniture. Black metal bottom with a Formica top—sturdy enough to last a millennium. On it sat a monitor, keyboard, a manila folder, and a few other files in a holder.

"How do you work like this?" I asked.

"Like what?" Isaac strolled past me, doughnut in hand, and reclined into his worn office chair.

I pointed toward his desk. "Where are all your files and papers? Aren't you doing any work?"

He held up the lone folder. "This is what I am working on. Just because my desk doesn't resemble your landfill of a work area doesn't mean I'm not doing anything." He chuckled. "So, what's up with your case?"

I filled him in on my grisly discovery in the forest. Isaac's face drew tight as I described the inhumane tactics and the fact that they were targeting endangered predators.

"This is my fifth find this winter. I have been reduced to following carrion signs. If it weren't for the crows circling the carcass, I'd have a hard time knowing where to look."

Isaac shook his head. "That's pretty bad. You have no leads on who it could be?"

"Nope. I can't even figure out how they are getting in and out so clean. The tracks lead straight to the animal and then out again. There's no tracking, no stalking. It's like they know exactly where the animal will be."

"Radio collars or GPS trackers?"

"No sign of either of those being used. Besides, I don't see these guys as being satisfied shooting a prize with a big tracker collar around its neck. Sure, they lame it, but a collar is so much less sporting because," I crinkled my nose in mock disgust, "then they have to see it."

Just trying to think the way they did made my stomach turn. As far as I was concerned, these *hunters* were about three steps off being serial killers.

"I did find some trail-cams, or at least a few spots where they were mounted, but I think they were there to watch the area more than track the animal."

Isaac rubbed the stubbly hair on his chin and stared at the ceiling. "I'm stumped. I haven't run into anything unusual either. Have you thought about running ballistics on the rounds they used?"

"So far that's turned out to be a bust. The lab is still analyzing what's left of the shells, but it looks like each kill is made with a different gun. Either we have a guy with a huge weapons stash, or this is a guide who takes out thrill seekers for the hunt of a life-time. I'm leaning toward the latter."

Isaac nodded. "I agree. If someone's out leading parties there, they must be getting business from someplace. I'll start sniffing around the web and see what I can turn up. Who knows? Maybe sickos like this have a website."

I laughed. "If they do, I owe you dinner."

"You owe me a round at that dive you hang out at and an introduction to your friend."

"What friend?" I asked.

Isaac made a face that looked somewhat constipated and a whole lot suspicious.

"You know what friend. The gorgeous brunette you always hang-out with but never make a move on."

"Oh, you mean Denise." I grinned

"Yes, Denise. That reminds me, I keep meaning to ask you.

And I mean this in the most respectful and supportive way. Are you gay?"

I narrowed my eyes and flipped Isaac a whole different sort of wild bird. "Not hitting on my friend doesn't mean I'm gay. Yes, she's … attractive, but she's my best friend. We talk, hang out, and have a good time, and that's it. I'm just not ready …"

"Look." Isaac sat forward and leaned in closer, lowering his voice in a sympathetic tone. "What happened to Susan was horrible. I know you miss her, and I won't even begin to say I understand. But it's okay to move on. You have a life to live. She would want you to be happy."

I nodded and tried not to snap off any number of angry retorts. He didn't understand. It was more than horrible. And being happy? Why did I deserve to be happy? I took a deep breath and refocused my pulsing emotions.

"I'll be happy when we catch the guys who are slaughtering these animals."

I stood up to leave, and Isaac got up with me. "Look, man, I'm sorry. I didn't mean to overstep. I just wanted to help."

"I know." I patted him on the shoulder on my way to the door. "Everyone wants to help. Let's just stick to something we can do and find these poachers instead."

CHAPTER SEVEN

My new protégé was waiting for me when I rounded the corner to my cubicle. She sat next to my desk, all pinched up like a nervous cat. The moment I appeared, she jumped up wringing her hands and invading my personal space with bags full of cheery thoughtfulness.

"Hi, Denise. I am so sorry this was ... I was sprung on you out of nowhere. I think Jim wanted it to be a good thing. Sort of a surprise. Like a puppy or a new dress." She smacked her forehead with the palm of her hand. "I can't believe I just compared myself to a puppy."

I almost cracked a grin at the sight of her. She was trying so hard her brain was about to explode. I had to give her credit. She reminded me of myself when I first started. Poor girl. She had no idea what she was in for.

I held up a hand to stop her, and she closed her mouth with an audible smack of her lips. "Our work day does not start until 9:00. It is now 8:30. Rule number one is no talking until the start of the work day. I am going to the restroom to change." I raised my eyebrows and tilted my head in her direction. "Someone in a yellow Volkswagen cut me off in traffic this morning and made me spill coffee all over my favorite skirt."

I took a step back and displayed the offending stain. The fact was, I hated the skirt. I had regretted even buying it and was almost grateful for an excuse to throw it away, but the three shades of green on Kacey's face made it my new favorite now.

"Coincidentally, that same car is parked in my spot downstairs. Could you inform the owner that parking in my spot again will force me to stink bomb her air vents and grease her windshield? If you can find the perpetrator, of course."

Kacey stared at me wide eyed, probably trying to decide whether or not I was serious. I wasn't, but she didn't know that. Let her wonder. I made a little lock and key motion at the corner of my mouth and then headed toward the ladies' room.

Inside was a small row of lockers where employees could keep a few personal things. I kept an emergency overnight bag complete with toiletries, makeup, a credit card, and a change of clothes. I have found almost every eventuality could be taken care of with these few items. If what I needed wasn't in my kit, I could always buy it with the card.

I wadded up my skirt and shoved it into the trash bin. Good riddance. A clean pair of navy-blue slacks hung in the locker and went perfectly with my blouse. I slipped them on then pulled out my makeup bag to set it on the sink in front of the mirror.

I was a mess. Mascara all down my face, lipstick smeared. It was no wonder Kacey was so scared of me. I looked like a bag lady serial killer. I snatched out a couple of tissues off the counter and cleaned up my face, then freshened up my makeup. When I looked presentable again, I closed my bag and tossed it back into the locker.

Good intensions or no, Jim still wasn't off the hook for this one. He had no business hiring someone to help me, especially without asking. Yes, this was his company, but how would he like it if someone hired an assistant to do all his dirty work? I crossed my arms, realizing how ridiculous that sounded. Any rational human being would like that just fine. In fact, Jim would probably be grateful— like I should be.

My reflection stared back at me in the mirror, weighing me down with judgment.

"Oh, shut up, you. That girl is going to home in on your territory, and you know it. So stop looking at me like that."

Even as I stared back at myself, I knew it wasn't true. Kacey was an over-eager girl looking for a start in a tough industry. I should go out there and guide her through the shark-infested waters. Or maybe just point at the sharks when they came to nibble at her tender bits.

I waited out the half hour in the bathroom until 9:00 rolled around. When I got back to my cubicle, Kacey still sat next to my desk. She looked a little more relaxed. Her legs were crossed, and her hands hung a bit awkwardly at her sides, as if she had practiced several other positions before settling on this one. To her credit, she let me get all the way into my work area and settled without saying a word. A consideration I appreciated after the morning's events.

"All right," I said, finally breaking the silence. "Jim wants me to fill you in on some of my clients, so let's start with the one coming in the morning. How much do you know about what we do here?"

Kacey cleared her throat and sat up, looking me in the eye with a confidence that surprised me. I hated that I liked this girl.

"I know you plan events for exclusive companies and high-end executives. You specialize in going the extra mile to provide an original experience and have clients from all over the world."

I raised an eyebrow. "Not bad. You read the web site." I paused and drew out the moment. She played with her pen, looking unsure of what to do next. "But what does that all mean? Do you know how much work goes into planning the elaborate events we pull off? We spend months contacting venues, coordinating entertainment, bringing in the right people, just to create the perfect event for a client. We strive for the illusion of effortless perfection above a mountain of baling wire, hard work, and duct tape. Is that what you want to do?"

Kacey nodded in quick, little jerks, making her red curls bounce up and down. "More than anything. You are the best in the business, and I want to learn from the best. I would have done it for free if Jim hadn't hired me."

I snorted. "Don't let Jim hear you say that, he might take you up on it."

Kacey let out a little laugh as well then stifled it with a cough. "Seriously, Denise. I'm sorry about how we met and how I came in here. All I want to do is help and learn everything I can along the way. Show me the ropes, and I promise I won't let you down."

I stared at her, trying not to grin, and shook my head. Eager to please and too innocent to know any better. Definitely, a younger me.

"All right." I pulled out a folder and plopped it down on my desk. "This is the information for Angelo Scalari's event. We are meeting him tomorrow morning. If we land his account, it will be one of the largest we have handled to date, and that is saying something."

I opened the file and fanned through the papers inside. "When he gets here, your job is to take notes, pay attention, and say nothing. Understand? If asks your opinion, say nothing. If he tells you he likes your shoes, say nothing. If he asks for your name ..."

"Say nothing," Kacey broke in. "I got it."

"No, tell him your name, for Pete's sake, we don't want him to think you are some kind of mute, but after that ..."

In unison we both recited the mantra. "Say nothing."

CHAPTER EIGHT

"Maybe it's not such a bad thing." Rob took a sip of his club soda as I poured myself another martini. Al had forgone the whole bartender routine and had just brought me the vodka, the vermouth, a shaker full of ice with a couple of olives on a napkin and told me to have at it.

"Of course it's a bad thing," I said. "He hired this girl to take the load off me. Now I have to work twice as hard to outdo her."

"I think you're looking at this the wrong way." He shot me a wary grin.

"There is no other way to look at it. There is one plate of food, and Jim wants us to share it. Sooner or later, one of us is going to get shoved out of the nest."

Rob gave me a crooked look.

"Oh, come on. You're a foresty guy. Don't you watch nature shows?" I added an olive to my drink. "There are always a bunch of baby birds, and the momma bird tries to feed them all. But there is this one little piggy bird who's always shoving the other birds out of the way. Before you know it, piggy bird's ass is the only thing that fits in the nest, the starving birdies are booted out, and Celine Dion is hosting an orphan bird infomercial."

Rob sat back in his chair with half a grin still painted on his face. "You might want to make that your last martini."

I huffed and downed half the drink. "I'm fine. She's just so, so, perky. She will be gunning for my job sooner or later. I hate her so much."

Rob laughed and pulled my drink out from in front of me. "You don't hate her. You like her, and it's driving you crazy. If you really hated this kid, you would chew her up and spit her out, not sit here and whine to me."

I sunk my forehead to the table with a clunk and let my arms hang toward the floor. "I know," I groaned. "What am I going to do?"

I sat like that for a moment, feeling the room spin a little with my eyes closed. Maybe Rob was right about the martinis.

After a few seconds, he tapped the back of my head as if he were knocking on a door. I lifted my gaze to his, blinking away the bleary fog.

"I'll tell you what you're going to do," he said. "You're going to show up tomorrow, do the same amazing job you always do, teach a new kid the ropes, and pass on some of the knowledge you have built up in that saucy little noggin of yours."

I smiled. "You always know the right thing to say."

He nodded. "What are friends for? Besides, I get to see you making a fool out of yourself, so it is sort of a win, win for me."

I reached out and tried to smack Rob's arm and missed by several inches. I looked at the half-empty martini glass and a pang of guilt rose in my stomach.

"Some friend I am. You have been dry for ... how long has it been now?"

"Fifteen months, two weeks, and three days. But who's counting?"

"Exactly. You pulled yourself together, and here I am, waving glass after glass of temptation under your nose."

"If I had a problem with it, I wouldn't be here."

There was a long silence between us. The kind where both people knew they should say something, but nothing seemed right. When I couldn't stand it anymore, I broke the stalemate.

"Letting go doesn't mean forgetting. You know that, right?" At least I could blame the awkward silence break on being drunk. "I miss Susan too. She was my best friend. I think about her every day. I will always remember her but—"

"I get it." Rob cut me off. "I need to let go. Thanks for the update."

I got ready to say something else when I heard a commotion. I turned to see a frat boy pull a wet bar towel off his face.

"What's the deal?" he said as he and his orange polo shirt-wearing buddy turned to face Al who stood across the bar.

The whole place went silent. It reminded me of an old western when some dumb upstart wandered in and annoyed the local gunslinger. Whatever happened, this would be good.

"The deal is," Al bellowed, "we have a strict no-drooling-windbag policy. Check the sign." He pointed over his shoulder to a wall occupied with nothing at all. "Even I can see the young ladies at that table don't want to be bothered. Trust me. I'm an expert on the subject."

Everyone in the bar looked like the audience at the Wimbledon open, shifting their eyes over to Frat Boy to see if he would return Al's volley.

"Screw you, man." He threw the bar towel on the floor. "That thing smells like feet."

Al shrugged. "Well, I used it to clean the toilet, so ..."

Frat Boy started to make a move toward Al, but Polo must have been the brains of the operation because he grabbed his arm and held him back. "Come on, man. Let's just go."

Frat Boy stared daggers at Al, who made comical little toilet cleaning gestures with his hands. "It was really disgusting. Had poo stains all over. I really had to get in there and dig it all out.

You can probably still see some of the schmutz on the towel there …"

I swore we were about to see Al go to work on this kid. Frat Boy's stupid meter was pegged almost as high as his pissed off meter. Polo knew it too. He wrapped an arm around his buddy's waist and pulled him toward the door.

"You two going dancing then?" Al raised a hand to wave at them. "All right. Have a good time."

Polo had to pull a little harder but managed to get his buddy out the door.

No one said a word as Al walked across the room and scooped up his towel from the floor.

One of the girls at the table cleared her throat. "Thank you, Mr. Grum, … umm, Al, sir."

He turned to look at them. "It's just Al." He started to walk toward the bar again and paused once more, waving the towel in his hand. "For the record, this is just chocolate, not … you know … poo."

Al made his way back to his spot behind the bar, clearly uncomfortable with the fact that he had just done his good deed for the day. Even if it had been at the expense of a couple of douchebags.

"Now that guy." I pointed at the bar. "I love almost as much as you."

Rob laughed. "You and me both."

The place went back to its quiet murmur of conversations while Rob and I nursed our drinks in silence. It was one of the great things between us. When we had something to say we said it. When we didn't, neither of us felt the need to fill the space with meaningless jabber.

After a few minutes, Rob set his glass down and looked over at me. "You're right."

I blinked at him. "Did I black out just then? Because I don't remember saying anything."

"No." Rob grinned. "About letting go. I've been thinking a lot about this lately, and I decided I'm going to sell the house."

I set my glass down on the table next to his. "Are you sure? That's a pretty big deal."

"No. And yes, it is. Something has to change. I feel like I need a big push to get myself moving, and right now, selling the house is it. Will you come help me pack?"

"You know I will."

"Thanks. How about day after tomorrow?"

"Perfect." I leaned in and covered his hand with mine. "I think this is going to be good for you, and I'll be there every step of the way."

"Thanks." Rob reached over and patted my hand with his. "I better get going. It's late, and I need to be up early."

"Actually, do you mind giving me a lift? I probably shouldn't be driving right now."

Rob leaned back in astonishment. "Denise, the night owl, turning in early? Are you feeling okay?"

"Shut up." I stood and brought my martini kit back to Al, then grabbed my coat off the chair. "I need to be in early if I'm going to outdo my new protégé. If she is even half as perky as I think she's is going to be, I'm going to need all the sleep I can get."

CHAPTER NINE

T he next morning, I pulled into the parking lot of my office building a full hour ahead of schedule. Eight in the morning was no ground-breaking hour to start the day, but no one would be in the office until nine. No one, that is, except Kacey Dubois.

Her yellow Bug, parked up in the front row of the lot, looked like a little baby chick wandering the vast expanse of blacktop. Part of me felt tempted to turn her car into a chicken nugget, but at least she wasn't in my spot.

I parked three slots down from her, and went into the building. I smoothed the collar on my pinstriped jacket and made sure my face was an impassive mask of stone when the doors to the elevator opened on my floor. Not a clack of a keyboard or the whirr of the copy machine could be heard. The least she could have done was get the coffee going. Then the heavenly aroma hit me. Coffee was already on. Another one for Kacey. Curse that girl.

I made my way to my cubicle and saw Kacey get up from her new desk to meet me. She walked in my direction with a pleasant expression on her face, but she didn't say anything. She reached for my coat, and I gave it to her as she walked by.

"Oh, Kacey, just so you know. We all have a sort of unofficial understanding about parking spots. You didn't park in mine today but ..."

When I turned around, I was surprised to see her standing there with a finger to her lips and shaking her perky little head back and forth. My voice trailed off as she offered a genuine smile and gestured toward the clock on the wall. I stared at it for a moment then looked back at her. She shrugged, bounced on her toes, then spun away without uttering a word of explanation.

My eyes went back to the clock again. Ten minutes after eight. Then it hit me. It wasn't nine o'clock yet. She had turned the no-talking-till-nine rule around on me. I narrowed my eyes and headed for my desk. I was losing ground fast, and Kacey hadn't even picked up any big guns.

Have it her way ... my way ... whatever. No talking till nine. I could use the peace and quiet anyway.

The next hour passed without seeing hide nor hair of my peppy sidekick. I went over my files on Angelo Scalari, typed up a few generic proposals, and watched as the usual trickle of office staff wandered in.

Jim had always believed in an open concept but still gave everyone their own space. I could see over each of the etched glass cubical dividers from my desk, allowing everyone to work in a team atmosphere or alone in their beautifully crafted desk space. All in all, it was a wonderful place to work. I just had to get over my merry little bump in the road.

"Good morning, Denise."

I all but jumped out of my pumps. Kacey appeared out of nowhere behind me, assaulting my ears with her greeting. "Geez, Kacey." I put a hand on my chest to calm my racing heart. "You shouldn't do that to people, especially before they've had their second cup of ..."

Coffee pot in hand, she reached over and refilled my mug. I glared up at her. Damn she was good.

"Sorry. I do that sometimes. My mom is always yelling at me for sneaking up on her, but I'm not even sneaking. I guess I'm just quiet. Maybe I should get some squeaky shoes or something. Then you would hear me coming for sure. Or a bell. My mom used to call me her little Tinkerbell when I was little —"

I held up a hand to stop her, afraid she might pass out from a lack of oxygen.

"Sorry. I guess I'm a little nervous." She took a step back. "Let me get rid of this."

I watched her bounce to the kitchenette to drop off the coffee pot, greeting everyone she passed with a big smile and a perky, "Good morning," before she made her way back to pull up a chair next to my desk. "What would you like me to do?"

"For starters, no more Mom stories. We'll save those for later." I shot her a tight-lipped grin. "Mr. Scalari should be here any minute. We'll head into the conference room and discuss what sort of event he is looking for. I will talk, and he will talk. And you will listen and take notes. If we need anything, it's your job to run out and get it. Can you handle that?"

"Got it."

"Denise?" I looked up to see our receptionist, leading a tall, sturdy looking man with thinning, graying hair. His eyes matched his impeccably tailored gray suit, and he moved with the confidence and grace of one accustomed to commanding a room.

"This is Mr. Angelo Scalari. Your nine o'clock."

I got out of my chair next to Kacey and held out a hand. "Mr. Scalari. It's so good to finally meet you. This is my assistant Kacey, and I'm Denise."

He reached out and shook both our hands in turn. "Please call me Angelo. This is a beautiful office."

"Just a taste of what we can offer in terms of an exclusive event for your guests." I flashed him an award-winning smile. "Shall we move over to the conference room where we can all be more comfortable?"

"No, this is fine." Angelo looked around the area and pulled a desk chair from a cubicle nearby. "I like things casual." He sat down and made himself comfortable, and Kacey followed suit, leaving me standing all by myself.

"All right. Here is good too." I sank back into my chair, trying to keep the sudden change in our meeting locale from putting me off my game. "I have a few examples here of other events we have hosted in the past." I fumbled with my file but couldn't seem to get the portfolio open in the smaller space and dropped it on the floor. I started to reach for it, wishing I could reset this morning, when he stopped me and reached for it himself.

"I don't need to see all that," he said as he handed me back the folder. "I always do my research. If I didn't think you could handle my account, I wouldn't be here."

I smiled, feeling a little more at ease with the compliment. "Thank you. We have worked with hundreds of executives over the —"

"Let me get right to the point," he interrupted again. "I have clients in town from all over the world. My business is tourism. My company provides journeys and experiences people can't find just anywhere. My previous event planner pulled out on me at the last minute. A legal complication that I won't go into. Short story is I need an original, over the top event planned and executed, and I need it done by this weekend."

I choked and squeaked out, "This weekend?" I glanced at Kacey who remained blissfully unphased as she continued to take notes.

"Like I said, my clients are already in town. I told them the location is a secret because the event is going to be big, and I don't want to spoil the surprise. All they need is an address."

My mouth hung wide open, but nothing came out except little grunts. It took me several seconds to even process what he had just requested. When I did, I couldn't help but laugh.

"Impossible. If we had several weeks to plan, maybe. But even then, events like this take months to put together. First, we have to find a location, then make sure it's available. Then there are the caterers, the decorations, the entertainment, and that is only the beginning. What you're asking for is … well, it's impossible."

Angelo sank back into his chair and rubbed his head. "I understand I'm asking for a lot, and I am willing to pay top dollar to make this happen. I had expected with your reputation …"

"You said you want something different?"

The two of us looked over at Kacey. She had her hand over her mouth, and her eyes were wide, obviously realizing she had broken the one rule I had set for her to follow.

"She just started yesterday. I'm sure —"

"No, please." He put his hand up to quiet me. I flinched and hoped neither of them noticed. I was losing ground, and I did *not* like it.

He looked at Kacey. "If you have an idea, I want to hear it."

Kacey looked over at me for conformation, and I gestured for her to continue. "Go ahead. We can't have the man thinking you are some sort of mute." Although, I was warming to the idea more and more.

Kacey sat up a little straighter and cleared her throat. "Well, I happen to know of a place in Breckenridge …"

"Out of town?" I exclaimed. "People like these want something in the heart of the city, not in a ski town."

"Please." Angelo held up a hand again. I growled inside. "Let her finish. I'm desperate, and my clientele like the outdoors. Remember I host adventure tours. What do you have for me, Kacey?"

"Like I said. There is this place in Breckenridge. It's brand new and hosts huge events. They have snowmobile tours, hiking, skiing, all sorts of stuff, then at night they finish the whole thing out in a club made entirely out of ice. It's pretty incredible."

"Sounds perfect." Angelo sat up in his chair and looked over at me. "Let's book this venue."

"Hold on a second." I held out my hands, feeling like I needed to slow things down for a moment so I could catch my breath and try to gain control. "Even if we could get the venue, which I doubt on this short of notice, there are still all the other details to consider."

Kacey cringed and held up her hand, waiting to be called on.

"We're not in class, you can just talk," I said through a forced smile.

"Actually, that's the beauty of this whole thing. My uncle owns the venue, and his son, my thoughtless cousin, stiffed him on a party. He stands to lose a bundle. All the infrastructure is already in place: caterers, a D.J., tour guides, the works. All I need to do is make a phone call, and we're set."

Angelo clapped his hands so loudly I nearly jumped out of my chair. At this rate, my heart was going to need a nap.

"Kacey, your uncle's deadbeat son may have saved the day." He laughed then stopped, no doubt realizing he had insulted a member of Kacey's family. "I'm sorry, I didn't mean ..."

"It's all right. He is a deadbeat. And I'll make the call—as long as it's all right with you, Denise."

I put on the best smile my strained, infuriated face could withstand without cracking. "Of course, Kacey. Set it up for tomorrow morning, and we will head up and take a look."

CHAPTER TEN

I pulled the forestry's flatbed truck around to the rear of the ranger station. My gruesome cargo was not only big, it was not something I wanted on display for every passing minivan and crossover full of kindergarteners.

"Looks like you've been busy." Isaac popped out the back door to the building, donning his flawless ranger hat. He was always a reverse image of me. Long sleeves and pants, always pressed drill sergeant sharp, and gleaming corfam shoes. A direct contrast to my short sleeves and muddy work boots. I wasn't afraid to get dirty. That was why I had landed this case, and it was getting dirtier by the second.

"How many did you get this time?" He walked around to the other side of the truck and unfastened the other end of the tarp that covered my cargo.

"Just one." I whipped away the heavy plastic, and he let out a long, slow whistle. "I had to come back to get the flatbed with a winch to haul him out."

"Is that what I think it is?" Isaac circled the truck, taking in the huge animal from every side.

"Was. Thought it might have been a big blackie, but even they don't get this big."

"So now your poachers are importing grizzly bears to the Rocky Mountains? What did they do, airlift this guy in? I've never seen a bear that big."

I pointed to the rear leg that extended all the way to the end of the flat bed. "Check out the wounds just above his back paw. The bone is broken too."

Isaac tried to lift the heavy appendage but only managed to shift it a little.

"Front paw is injured too. This poor guy was barely moving when they caught up to him."

Isaac spit off to the side. "What kind of lowlife does this to an animal?"

I shook my head. "I don't know, but I'm going to find out. I want these guys so bad; I can taste it. At least they put him out of his misery. I counted at least twenty entry wounds. I stopped looking after that."

"That reminds me. Ballistics got back to me with the results of that wolf you brought in. Not good news. They used Remington .223 rounds. Best guess is they hunted with AR-15s."

I sighed. "Great. A whole party of illegal poachers toting ARs with no conscience. Just what I want to run into when I'm all alone in the woods."

"That's no joke." Isaac leaned against the truck still eyeing the mountain of matted fur and blood. "These guys are dangerous. Anyone willing to go to all this trouble and expense wouldn't think twice about wasting a Ranger out in the middle of nowhere."

I nodded. "Maybe I can catch them someplace more convenient. Do you think they would come down to the station if we asked real nice? I could leave them a note or something."

"Don't be an ass," Isaac said. "You know I'm right. You need to be careful. Maybe it's time you call in some state help."

"What am I going to tell them? I need fifty troopers to stake out the forest for endangered species?" I threw up my hands. "I'm still resorting to following the crows to the carcasses. Ballistics can't tell me anything other than I am facing military grade hardware, and these guys are so good even I have a hard time finding their tracks. What I need is a lead, and I can't dig one of those up with a seven-foot shovel."

I slumped against the truck and stared at the poor beast next to Isaac. "These guys are slick. They use hunting season to cover their shots, and they're in and out like cats. Even backtracking from the kill, it's hard to find prints, and I have yet to find one defined enough to cast. They go in quick, hit their mark, and get out. They know how to cover their trail and have some heavy fire power. I feel like I'm up against Special Forces, not a bunch of thrill seekers."

Isaac dipped his head in thought. "I wish I could help you more. No one has seen anything suspicious. I have every Ranger Station in the area on alert. But without more to go on, that's all I can do."

"I appreciate it. If you hear anything let me know."

"I will, and I'm serious about being careful. Watch yourself out there. You need backup, call me."

I clapped him on the shoulder. "Thanks. You know," I paused to glance down at his feet. "If I call, you might have to actually go outside and get those pretty shoes dirty."

Isaac looked down too. "That's all right. I keep half a dozen of these in my closet. One scuff, and they're out the door."

I laughed. "Make sure you have them ready. Wouldn't want you looking like you work for a living."

"I leave all that dirty work for you. I've moved into the twenty-first century. You know we have computers now."

"Computers can't track poachers through a forest."

"No, but computers don't die when you shoot them either."

I raised an eyebrow at him. "I would beg to differ."

Isaac blinked, realizing the lunacy of his statement. "You know what I mean. Just be careful. I don't want someone hauling you in on a flatbed truck."

I nodded. "Nor do I, my friend, nor do I."

CHAPTER ELEVEN

"A bear?" The words came out louder than intended, and I glanced around Grumpy's to see if the other dozen or so patrons in the bar had heard me. Nope. I went back to tearing another corner off the little cocktail napkin I was in the process of mutilating and set it on the growing pile in front of me, next to my water glass. "Like … a real bear?"

Rob nodded. "We don't have grizzlies here in the Rockies. Not officially, anyway. People have reported seeing them but nothing substantiated."

"You mean like Bigfoot?" I asked.

Rob laughed. "Kind of, except Grizzlies are real. They just shouldn't be in our neck of the woods. They're on the endangered species list along with the two gray wolves I found. These jerks started with a lynx and a couple of cougars. Probably perfecting their stalking techniques."

I tore off another corner and added it to the pile. "I had no idea you did stuff like that. I really thought it was just, you know …"

"Bringing the hammer down on big, bad fishermen?"

My gaze went to the table. "Well, when you say it like that, it sounds silly."

"These guys are serious. They're armed with military grade weapons and target endangered animals for the fun of it. Right now, they're getting away with it because I can't get any kind of lead on them." Rob had his big hands clenched into fists on top of the table. "If I don't find a way to sniff them out, they're going to keep doing it. God forbid they move on before I get my hands on them. They may never get caught."

A metal shaker slammed down onto the table making me jump and let out a small screech. I looked up to see Al standing over us wearing a bright yellow Hawaiian shirt.

"What is it with people scaring me today?" I said trying to rein in my nerves.

He swayed a bottle of vodka and vermouth in each hand. "Looked like you might need something stronger than water, judging from the napkin volcano you're building."

I looked down at the table and saw that my little pile had grown into a mountain of shredded paper. I slapped my hand over it, causing the delicate structure to woosh out in every direction.

"Subtle," Al whispered, then much louder, "So how 'bout it. A little elixir to take the edge off?"

I smiled. "What has you in such a good mood that you're actually bringing a drink to us? And you look so ... sunny. I'm beginning to like the yellow shirt."

"Yeah, well, don't get used to it. The service, not the shirt. Saw a rollover accident this morning on the way to the bank. A honey wagon jumped the curb and hit a garbage truck. No one was hurt, but it cracked the sewage tank like an egg. The stench was horrendous, but it made me think. Yeah, I woke up this morning, cut myself six times shaving, ran out of beer for my cereal, and only had this eye-searing shirt to wear, but things could be worse. I could've met my end on that corner covered in crap and rotted cabbage." Al smiled and waved his bottles again. "But instead, I'm chatting with you lovely folks while you loiter, drinking free water in my bar."

I looked over at Rob. He shrugged and shot me a sideways grin. "How can you resist an invitation like that?"

"It appears I can't." I glanced back up at Al and smiled back at him. "Pour away."

Al started to tip the bottles then lost his grin as a pair of boisterous patrons got a little too excited about the game they were watching and knocked over a table full of drinks.

He jammed the bottles down on our table. "Help yourself. Looks like I need to go see to a cleanup."

As soon as the jolly duo saw Al coming, they righted the table and started piling glasses up so fast I thought they might start grabbing them from other tables as well.

"I'm sorry I unloaded all that on you. I didn't mean to make you worry. I know how to handle myself. Nothing bad's going to happen."

"I'm not worried," I lied. "You'll figure this out one way or another. Just be careful. I can't imagine how empty my life would be without you in it."

The admission fell out of nowhere, and Rob stared at me, mouth half open as if he wanted to speak but couldn't.

"As friends I mean." I stuttered out the words and shook my head, unable to meet his eyes. "Maybe I do need this drink."

I grabbed the bottles on the table, opened the shaker and poured a healthy serving of vodka over the ice, then added the vermouth. I shook the contents, then realized I had no glass.

Rob seemed to realize it too and got up before I could move. "I'll get it."

He was away in a flash, and I watched as he almost collided with one of the patrons from the overturned table who was now running across the bar with a mop.

Where had that come from? My life would be empty without

you in it? True statement, but not one you made to your buddy. Not in Grumpy's Happy Shack, anyway.

I shook my head and blew it off. Rob knew what I meant. After all, a girl had a right to say something girly every once in a while.

"Your glass, ma'am." He set a martini glass down, complete with three olives impaled on a tiny plastic sword, and sank back into his chair. "I think Al's going to have those guys buff the floor before the night's over."

I poured my drink. "Love that guy," I said.

"You and me both." Rob eyed me, and I could tell he was going to say something about my comment. I figured I better head him off instead.

"It's too bad you can't use the sheriff department's helicopter to search for your guys. Seems like it would be a lot faster than driving around."

Rob laughed. "I wish it were that easy. They would hear the chopper coming from miles away. Disappearing in the woods wouldn't be too hard for a small group of hunters wearing camouflage."

I shrugged. "At least you could get in to catch them faster."

Rob started to nod, then the smile fell away from his face. "Denise, you are a genius."

I raised an eyebrow. "Thanks?"

Rob stood up and pulled on his coat. "I have to go. Will you be all right? Can I give you a lift home?"

"I'm a big girl," I said, still a little startled by his sudden attitude shift. "I'll be fine. Go do your crazy catch-the- poachers-park-ranger thing."

"Okay." Rob hurried toward the door, glancing back to wave goodbye. "I'll see you tomorrow. Don't forget. My place, after work."

I waved back. "Got it. Now get out of here." I smiled.

Rob ran out the door.

"But you better come back to me," I whispered and took a drink. He really was a big part of my life—my best friend. The thought of him running into assholes with guns and getting hurt had me choking down the threat of tears. What was with me today? Probably Kacey and the one power bar I had today. I would have to eat better if my emotions kept popping up like this. Two power bars at least.

CHAPTER TWELVE

Isaac picked up one of the printouts I had spread across the desk in his office. "Drones?"

"I was up half the night studying them. I got the idea from a friend. Actually, she mentioned helicopters, but it jogged this little gem out of my brain."

"She?" Isaac waggled his eyebrows at me. "Would we be talking about your gorgeous and conspicuously available friend?"

I sighed. "Yes, it was Denise. Could we just keep our minds on the case, creeper? You wouldn't believe how much information I had to slog through to find this. I can never unlearn all the stuff I picked up in that geekdom."

Isaac laughed. "Fine, but I still don't get it. What do drones have to do with the poachers?"

Isaac held up a photo of one of the elite models I had found on the internet.

"What you are holding in your hand is not only their way in and out, but their tracking system and lookout too."

Isaac turned the picture back toward him so he could scrutinize it again. "I thought these things had a limited range. My nephew has a pretty nice one, and it only lasts about twenty minutes before the battery dies. And he has to have a line of sight to fly it."

"I'm sure your nephew has a nice little rig, but these things are on a whole other level. Like thirty to forty grand sort of level."

Isaac whistled and shook his head. "That's crazy. Why would anyone spend that kind of money on a mini helicopter?"

"These machines have a flight time of better than ninety minutes and can reach a range exceeding twenty-five miles. Plenty of time to track a lamed animal and lead a hunting party into and out of an area, especially if they're working with more than one drone."

"So, you think they're bringing the animal in, trapping it until they're ready, then they follow it with a drone until the hunting party shows up to get their jollies? That's pretty diabolical."

I nodded. "The only way to get that kind of range is to use low frequency transmitters. Most are supposed to be limited to a mile or so, but our guys have to be reaching way past that."

I pulled out a sheet from the bottom of the file covered in numbers and calculations. "This is the part where I am reaching a little bit."

"This is this part where you're reaching?" He raised his eyebrows. "Not the evil drone UFO theory? That wasn't reaching?"

"All right, this is where I am reaching a little more." I flipped the paper around to face him and pointed to a series of numbers in the center of the page. "There is a sweet spot right here, frequency wise, that I bet they are using. Get too low and you run into cellular telephone ranges. Too high and you start to lose range. But right here," I pounded the paper on the desk with my finger again for punctuation. "Right here is a frequency reserved for military use only. Now, if there is no military in the area to catch them, this frequency range would be a free playground for the kiddies and their evil UFO drones."

"And you want to track the frequency. That's pretty high tech for an old trail beater." Isaac laughed.

"You are way older than I am."

"Maybe so, but I'm pretty. You just have all that," he waved his hand in my direction, "rugged manliness slapped all over your face."

"Fine. You're a pretty old guy. Can we get back on subject?"

He narrowed his eyes at my play on words, and I went on before he could formulate a retort.

"To answer your question, yes. If I can find a way to scan for this frequency range, I should know the moment they launch. If I have a way to track the signal, I should be able to follow it right back to the source."

"You may not be reaching as far as you think," Isaac said. "I have a buddy who works down in Golden. He does radio maintenance for all our Forestry rigs. He is a huge HAM radio nut in his off time and works as a fox hunter on the side."

I raised an eyebrow wondering what hunting foxes had to do with tracking my drones.

Isaac let my confusion hang for a moment then sighed. "He uses radio tracking equipment to hunt down malicious radio transmissions designed to disrupt emergency channels and public broadcasting sites. I'd bet dollars to dingo's he could rig up something that would work for you."

I smiled, feeling some relief that I may have a genuine lead. "What are we waiting for? Let's go see him."

Isaac held out his hand. "Hold on a second. We can't just go barging in on him. He's a busy man. Besides you have that other problem."

"What problem?" I looked down at the paperwork on his desk wondering if my late-night research session had caused me to forget something.

"I'm not sure a *pretty old guy* like me can remember my friend's phone number." He squinted at the old, green landline perched on his desk. "I'm pretty sure there was a seven in it." He made his voice turn all wobbly. "Or was that a Q? Heavens to Betsy, I feel so feeble I can barely hold myself up."

I eyed his old man routine and sighed. "Would lunch at Bob's Atomic Burgers help you to gain your strength back, Grandpa?"

Isaac popped up to his feet, and he snatched his hat off the desk. "I think that'd about do it, Sonny. Let's get going. We can call my buddy after we eat."

CHAPTER THIRTEEN

"You have got to be joking." It took every last fiber of self-control to keep myself from kamikazeing my car into Kacey's yellow butter bomb. She had parked it in the farthest part of the parking lot in a spot right next to the main road. Part of me wondered if she left it there to be sure I wouldn't miss it. A little poke to announce she had beat me to work again and parked in a spot no sane person would ever use. She must have walked a mile just to get to the front doors, and now every delinquent on the street would see her bright yellow bullseye just asking to be vandalized.

A pang of guilt threatened to weave its way into my throat, and I let out a frustrated groan. Why did she have to be so ... nice? It would be so much easier if I *wanted* someone to break into her car. Now I would have to try and keep her from becoming a city statistic.

I pulled into my spot and threw my door open. The seatbelt was still buckled, so when I stepped out, the strap tried to strangle me. I groaned and reached back to undo it, but somehow my arm got tangled in the belt. When I tried to yank it free, my elbow rammed itself into the doorjamb. I threw my head back in pain, crying out a little curse only to follow up my elbow with a bashed skull on the door frame.

Karma. Sometimes her sense of humor was just too much to take.

I stopped moving and untangled the spiderwebbed trap that ensnared me. The car door slammed with a dull thud, and I rubbed my elbow and my head at the same time.

The aches felt a little better by the time I got off the elevator and so had my sour mood. I headed in toward my cubicle and scanned the office for any sign of Kacey. If I were going to do my good deed for the day, I wanted to get it over with early.

It wasn't long before I saw her rounding the corner from the break room, no doubt fresh from percolating a perfect pot of coffee to go with the delicious homemade Danish crafted from a recipe handed down from her ancient ancestors.

I started to say something about her parking choice, but I was stopped short when I saw her outfit. A simple green blouse, jeans, and tennis shoes. I had decided on a more casual outfit today, opting for slacks, a cardigan, and heels, but she looked as if she were ready to head out for a weekend picnic.

My mouth opened to say something, which I'd probably regret, but Kacey smiled and pointed to her watch before I could utter a single syllable. I clapped my mouth shut again and shook my head. My damn, no-talking-before-nine rule was beginning to irritate *me*.

I held out a hand before she could get past me. "Look, today maybe we make a little exception to our agreement."

Kacey's face lit up with so much joy I immediately wanted to change my mind.

"That's great. I hate not being able to say hello to you in the morning. It just feels so cold, don't you think? Did you see where I parked this morning? I hope that's all right. I figured that would be a good place to park Miss Daisy. Plus, it helps me get my steps in for the day."

"About that," I began. "you should probably move it away from ... wait, Miss Daisy?"

"Yeah. I named her that because she's yellow. I thought about Tweety or Princess Buttercup, but I wanted something totally original, you know?"

"So, you're driving Miss Daisy?"

Kacey just smiled and nodded. "Yup. What do you think?"

"I think it's amazing," I said. "But there's been some vandalism around here lately. So if you want to keep your car in one piece, you should be *driving Miss Daisy* away from that main street as soon as you get a chance."

This time I annunciated the key words low and slow.

Kacey blinked. Nothing.

"Okay, thanks for the advice. I'll get her moved here in a little bit."

I smacked my forehead as she walked away. Everything inside me itched to explain, but she couldn't have missed the reference. Was she toying with me? If so, I had to give her credit. She was good. I resisted my every urge to swallow the bait and turned to address her before she got too far away.

"Kacey, one more thing."

She stopped and turned to face me, the same gleeful smile on her face.

"About what you're wearing. We try to—"

The elevator doors opened behind her, and I saw Angelo Scalari step out. He wore jeans, tennis shoes, and a green sweater that matched Kacey's so close in color they could have come from the same dye lot.

My jaw tightened, and I felt my eye twitch. How had she known? She picks today of all days to come in dressed like Cathy the Queen of Casual, and her outfit just happens to match our client's right down to the color of his shirt? If I didn't get back on my game soon, I would be forced into an early retirement. That, or a nervous breakdown, one or the other.

I raised a hand and forced a practiced smile on my face. "Angelo. You're early. Welcome. Are you ready for our big trip to the mountains?"

Kacey spun around, and I braced myself for the inevitable revelation. She let out a laugh and pointed at him. "Twinsies!"

Angelo smiled back at her. "I have to complement you on your attire, young lady." He leaned in when he got close to Kacey as if he were telling her a secret, but he didn't lower his voice. "Maybe we should talk to Denise about loosening up a little bit. You should give her some pointers."

We all laughed, and I imagined shoving a dirty sock in Kacey's mouth.

"I think we're ready whenever you are. We just need to gather our files and then we can head out."

Kacey nodded. "I'll go get them, and our coats, and meet you back here at the elevator."

She skipped away, and Angelo shook his head. "You must be happy to have found someone like her. She's really on the ball."

I nodded. "I count my lucky stars every single day."

Angelo turned his gaze to me and smiled. "By the way, I have a little surprise for you. I hope you don't mind if I provide the transportation up today. The weather is beautiful, and I wanted to blow the cobwebs out of one of my old cars."

"That sounds perfect. What kind of car is it?"

"It's a secret." He smiled.

"I love old cars. Actually, it's a bit of a hobby for me."

"Really?" He seemed surprised.

"My dad always worked on classic cars. He even left me one when he passed away. I still have it in storage. It's a 1954 Mercury Monterey convertible. Canary yellow with red interior. It's pretty amazing."

"Wow. That is a real piece of art. I'd love to see it sometime."

I shrugged. "I haven't taken it out in years. I pay a mechanic to look after it. Keep it running and all, but I never have time to get out and drive it. I'm always here."

"There's more to life than working. You should make time to enjoy it. I'll bet your dad would want you out driving that car."

I looked down, feeling the shame of knowing he was right.

"I'm sorry. I didn't mean to step out of line."

"You're fine. Sometimes I hear a bit of his voice in other people, that's all."

Angelo smiled. "Well, I think you are going to enjoy my little surprise. Shall we call the elevator? So we are ready when Kacey gets back?"

"Sure. If she misses it, she'll find her way down one way or another."

CHAPTER FOURTEEN

Angelo's little secret as it turned out, was not so little. It was a stretched 1939 Cadillac Series 75. If Dick Tracy were alive, he would have overdosed on the cool factor and driven it all the way to gangster heaven.

"Wow … just … wow." I was speechless. I ogled the automotive art while Angelo stood half a pace behind me. It was midnight black, had long, bullet style headlights, enough chrome in the grill to blind oncoming aircraft, and suicide rear doors over the running boards. If there were a more awesome limo in existence, it had to be on another planet.

"I'm glad you like it. Found her rusting out in an old junkyard and resurrected the bones into this. I kept it authentic as I could to the time."

"You did an incredible job. I have never seen anything like it."

Kacey caught up to us clasping a set of file folders to her chest. She wore her coat and had mine draped over her arm. "Is that a thirty-nine Cadillac?"

I turned to face her, stunned into silence for a second time.

Angelo answered with a slow nod. He looked almost as astounded as I felt. "Yes, it is. Do you know cars?"

She shrugged her shoulders. "Sort of a hobby. I love old hotrods and lead sleds. I am going to have one of my own someday."

I wasn't sure if I was pleasantly surprised or overly appalled that Kacey and I had something in common. Either way, I wasn't going to let it spoil my ride in the vehicle of the century.

"Shall we?" I looked to Angelo, and he made a motion toward the car. The dark tinted windows obscured any view to the interior, so I hadn't noticed the driver until he opened the door. When the chauffer stepped out, all garbed out in an early twentieth century suit, tie, and a wide brimmed fedora, an excited little giggle escaped my throat.

"You really go all out," I said.

"Color me guilty of trying to impress two beautiful ladies."

Now it was Kacey's turn to giggle. Angelo was old enough to be her father, mine too for that matter. Giggling at a comment like that sent all the wrong messages.

I just smiled and nodded, accepting the compliment at face value as I stepped toward the open door held by the chauffer.

Kacey took off her coat, then hopped out in front of me and crawled inside, scurrying to the far end of the rear facing seat. I made my way in behind her and sat in the seat facing her. Everything inside was upholstered in baby-soft, beige leather, trimmed out with walnut and gold accents. It was like stepping into a miniature 1920s nightclub. Everything was time period appropriate down to the liquor bottles nestled between the seats in the wet bar.

Angelo ducked into the car with a smile on his face and sat next to me. "Well, what do you think? Will this get us up to the mountain and back?"

"It'll do," I said. "Maybe next time we should bring Kacey's Bug so we can all have a little more room."

Angelo laughed and so did Kacey. I was glad she took it as lighthearted as I had intended.

The car started moving, and I reached down out of instinct, looking for my seatbelt.

"Something wrong?" Angelo caught me digging around in my seat as if I were starving to death and had just lost my last gobstopper.

"Sorry. Just looking for my seatbelt. Sort of a habit, I guess."

"This is a '39. I don't think they had even heard of seatbelts back then," he said. "If it makes you feel any better, this thing is built like a tank. If we hit something, we are more likely to go through it than get stopped by it."

I let out an uneasy laugh and nodded. "It's fine. Like I said, just force of habit." I did my best to resituate myself and look comfortable, but the thought of riding hours without a seatbelt made my insides want to backflip. I knew it was silly. Chances were, everything would be fine. No one needed a seatbelt when things were fine, they were made for the times when they weren't fine.

I let out a gentle sigh and did my best to quiet the images of horrible accidents playing out in my mind. Angelo and Kacey were already talking, and I fretted over a seatbelt. If Rob were here, he would understand. He would remind me about it every three minutes with fiery statistics of car crashes just to watch me hyperventilate but at least he would understand. He knew me better than anyone.

Why was I thinking about Rob? Get your head in the game, Denise. What is wrong with you? Forget the seatbelt, forget Rob, you have a client to win.

"The numbers here look pretty high," Angelo said. "I hold this event every year, and I have never spent this kind of money."

"Unfortunately, our options have been cut pretty short this time," I interjected. "The timeline we need to adhere to and the unusual setting you requested have made it difficult to find anything at all."

Angelo's eyes went back down to the price sheet Kacey had provided, and he nodded with a grimace.

"If you're still interested in a downtown venue, I made a few phone calls yesterday." I had saved this little surprise for the perfect moment. "I found a hotel venue willing to host your event for a very reasonable price. It won't be as extravagant as what Kacey has arranged, but the hotel has agreed to cover everything, including the lodging of your guests. And it is right off 16th street downtown."

Angelo's eyebrows went up at that. He thought about it for a minute then shook his head. "No. If this place is everything Kacey says it is, price is no object. I have a reputation to uphold, and my clients shouldn't have to sacrifice for my previous event planner's mistakes."

"Excellent." I gave him a tight-lipped smile. "Then it sounds like were still on the right track."

"I have a surprise too," Kacey said. "When I told my uncle who you are and what you do, he seemed very excited to work with you. After all, you are sort of in the same business. You host adventure tours; he has an adventure destination. I think he's hoping you and your clients like the place enough to come back again."

"I hope I like it too," Angelo said, "but I don't understand how that's a surprise."

Kacey shook her head as if trying to jostle the right words out of her brain. "The rates I shared are those he would charge his regular clients. You have to understand those prices aren't just for a party, which, don't forget, is in a big castle made of ice, but it's also for a whole weekend of skiing, snowmobiling, hiking, snow-shoeing, and lots of other things. For you, he is pulling out all the stops on a one-day event for a quarter the price."

Even my jaw dropped at that little tidbit of information. "A quarter the price, on this short of notice? How did you get him to —"

"I cheated." She laughed. "I used the family connection. He would have never given it to me otherwise. Not for that price anyway. And like I said, it's great for him because he gets exposure to a whole new set of clients." She paused a moment then added. "Plus, it helps that his deadbeat son backed out on his event at the last minute. Like I told you earlier, he stood to lose a bundle before we came along to save the day."

I nodded. "Nice work, Kacey." It amazed me how fast she could go from fingernails on a chalkboard to pure brilliance.

"Nice work indeed." Angelo closed the folder on his lap and reached forward to the little bar between the seats. He pulled out what looked like a bottle of bathtub bourbon and uncorked the top. "True to the vehicle we're riding in, this is a genuine sample of Old Forester prohibition-style bourbon. They still make it today, and I figured what better to toast our futures together." He poured three glasses and offered one to each of us.

"To our annual events." He raised his glass, and we all clinked them together. "May they all be exciting, adventurous, and seventy-five percent off."

We all laughed and took a sip of the straight whiskey. Kacey and I coughed while Angelo twisted his head in fiery discomfort.

"Perhaps we will stop somewhere and find some champagne to toast our success on the way back."

Kacey ventured one more sip and held her glass on her knee. "At least we won't be cold when we get out of the car. This stuff would light a penguin on fire."

Angelo was taking another sip of his own and almost spit it all over the car. He swallowed and let out a huge belly laugh. "I have been looking for a logo for my company. I think you may have just stumbled upon the winner."

I smiled at a multitude of strange images that popped into my mind and shook my head. Kacey really had a knack for this sort of thing. Much as I was beginning to like her, my career may be in more trouble than I had thought.

CHAPTER FIFTEEN

"Thanks for running me up to the lookout station." Isaac relaxed in the passenger seat of my Jeep, spinning a toothpick between his lips and looking about as content as a cat sunning in a window. "I've been meaning to get up here for weeks."

"It's the least I can do," I said. "Especially after you got your buddy, Jerry, to work on my tracker so fast. I can't believe he's going to have something put together by tomorrow."

Isaac sat up and grabbed hold of the roll bar as I pulled off the highway and onto the off-road trail that led to the lookout station. "It was nothing. That lunch at Bob's Atomic Burgers was payment enough for three favors. Besides, Jerry probably has something built already. Half-way there anyway. He loves that stuff so much I'm sure he'd pay you to let him build it."

I laughed and steered around a big rock in the middle of the trail. The Jeep bounced, and we both came off our seats.

"This ain't a race, you know. We're just going up to grab a broken antenna array for Jerry. He will be there tomorrow, whether my kidneys are working or not."

I laughed again as we hopped over a small rise and squeezed

past some low hanging pine branches. "What fun is it to drive off road if you crawl along like an old lady?" The needles scraped along the side of the jeep, and Isaac leaned in toward the middle as if they were going to reach in to grab him.

"I would just like to get there and back in one piece, that's all. You can barely see what's under the snow."

I dropped my head in defeat and let off the accelerator, slowing to a senior citizen speed. "This better for you? If you like, we could get out and walk. Or would that be a little too zippy for you?"

Isaac let go of the roll bar and settled back into his seat again. "This'll be just fine, sonny. Walking makes my bunions hurt."

I shook my head, and we made our way up the mountainside at a slightly faster pace than a snail might run the hundred-yard dash. The farther we went up, the deeper the snow got. The trees thinned, and the pine forest gave way to rocky tundra. It took us almost an hour to snake our way through the fresh powder to the forestry gates and up to the little cabin that overlooked the valley.

"I can't remember the last time I was up here." I turned off the engine, and we both stepped out into the cold. "I almost forgot about how beautiful it is."

I looked out at the expanse of snowy mountain peaks and deep, green valleys. It was as if life had come together just to paint this silent masterpiece.

"That's what you get for being all uppity with your ISB badge. You need to get out here with us regular rangers every once in a while. Too much of that special investigations stuff is toxic for the soul."

I nodded and squinted out at the view. "You're probably right."

"I'll just be a second. The antenna's already down. I'll go grab it and put it in the back."

I waved by way of response and basked in the calm silence of the mountain. There wasn't a cloud in the clear, blue sky. The sun shone off the snow-covered trees below, shimmering like a million tiny diamonds nestled in cotton. It was a rare moment when the whole world seemed to stop and appreciate the power and magnificence of nature.

Denise would love this. A memory shot into my mind of a time we went to the mountains for a Saturday picnic about a year after Susan had died. I somehow convinced her to take the day off from work and spend it with me. We found the perfect spot, like this one, and spent hours talking, sharing memories of Susan, and admiring the incredible view. She had seemed so relaxed. It was great day, and it made me wish we made time for more.

"You having a seizure or something?" Isaac's voice broke through my euphoria like a garbage truck with squeaky brakes. "Get over here and help me."

I turned to see him struggling with several pieces of a large antenna. They were all jumbled in his hands and about to teeter off and disappear into the snow. I went to meet him halfway, but something across the valley caught my eye. I stopped and tried to spot it again but couldn't pick it out among the trees.

"Rob! Seriously. Can you at least open the back of the Jeep?"

I spun and hurried over to help him with the mass of tangled metal in his hands. "Sorry. I thought I saw something out there."

I opened the back, and Isaac piled everything in. "Probably just bigfoot. That guy's been hanging out up here for years."

I shook my head and hurried to grab the binoculars out of my glove compartment. By the time I had them out, Isaac was standing next to me.

"What are we looking for?" He had his hands up, shielding the sun out of his eyes. "Can you give me a clue? Is it bigger than an Atomic Bacon Burger?"

I ignored Isaac's comments and scanned the far mountainside below. The chances that it was actually ...

"There!" I pointed slightly to the left and down to a valley on the opposite side. "Do you see it?"

Isaac stepped forward and squinted in the same direction. "What are you talking about? I don't see anyth ..." He took a few more steps as if getting closer would help him see better. "Can't be. I've never seen one that big."

"Yes, you have." I scrambled back to the Jeep and slammed the back doors closed. "The drones I showed you earlier look just like that one. To get the lift and range they need to spot the animals, it has to be that big. Get in."

Isaac hurried back to the passenger side and jumped in just as I got the motor running again. "What are you going to do? The trail backtracks the other way. We'll never get down and around in time."

"Put on your seatbelt, Grandpa. We're not going to backtrack. We're going to catch that thing."

Isaac started to say something else, but his voice cut off in a chirped little yell as I floored the accelerator and headed straight down the mountain.

"Are you crazy?" His voice came out high and cracked as he struggled with the buckle. "You are going to get us killed."

"It's snow. It'll break our fall. Don't worry. Just keep your eyes peeled for that drone."

We picked up speed, and the chassis rattled like a jackhammer as we sped over the uncut wilderness. Snow flew up in rooster tails of fine powder as I turned, snaking through trees and avoiding boulders. I tried the brakes once, but even touching them turned us into the world's heaviest toboggan. I decided not to let Isaac know about that little development.

The Jeep swerved from side to side like a speed skier. It was all I could do just to maintain control. Isaac might have been right about one thing. Okay, maybe two things. This was definitely crazy, and there was such a thing as too fast when you drove off-road.

We careened toward a thick stand of trees, so I cranked the wheels and gave it some gas. Good news—the lower we went, the less snow there was, making it easier to see the ground. Bad news—the lower altitude meant more trees, and they were getting thick fast. It wouldn't be long before the ratio between slick ground and speeding tree trunks would be too much to handle.

I saw a spot where the trees thinned out to a clearing, and I headed for it. "Do you see it anywhere?" I called out above the screaming engine and rattling wheels.

"You mean do I see the drone through all these trees and the blizzard of snow you're spraying into the air? No, you lunatic. The Hubble Telescope couldn't find it through all this."

"Hold on a second."

"What else am I going to do? And by the way, as soon as you stop, I'm going to throw up all over your floor."

I threaded the vehicle through another stand of trees, clipping the mirror on Isaac's side. He let out a screech as the ground leveled out from freefall to quadruple black diamond. I pumped the brakes, and they slowed the Jeep in the ever-thinning snow cover. The clearing was just past the trees ahead. If I got us through there, maybe we could get another lead on the drone and —

"Stop!" he yelled.

My adrenaline already hovered at eleven, so Isaac's panicked voice almost made me fly out of my seat. I swerved to the left and hit the brakes hard. The tires found dirt and dug in. Gravity spun us around, and we came to a halt not three feet from where I intended to break through the tree cover to the clearing.

Isaac threw open the door and all but fell out.

"What's wrong? What are you doing?" Panic began to take a backseat to frustration. "This might be my best shot at catching these guys! Get back in!"

Isaac leaned against the hood of the Jeep for a minute then looked up at me with furious eyes. He marched around to my door, threw it open, and grabbed me by the shoulder. For a minute, I thought he was going to hit me, but he just pulled me out far enough so I could turn around and look behind us.

"You want to keep heading that way, you're going to have to do it without me." He pointed at the opening in the stand of trees where I had intended to break through. Now that we weren't hurling through the forest, I could see why Isaac was so upset.

The area I thought was a clearing was no clearing at all. The reason there were no trees was because there was nothing there. It was a drop-off so deep I couldn't even see the treetops below. A few more feet, and it would have been too late. I would have recognized my mistake in time to know I had doomed us both. If it hadn't been for Isaac, that crazy chase down the mountain would have been our last, and Denise would have never forgiven me for never making it home.

CHAPTER SIXTEEN

The two-hour ride up to Breckenridge in Angelo's plush limo was filled with pleasant conversation and cocktails. When our driver pulled the stretched '32 Cadillac into the dirt parking lot, the car's engine hummed to a smooth halt, and the suicide door opened, allowing a torrent of bright sunlight and pine mountain air to invade the cabin. Angelo gestured for me to exit, so I did my best to steady my wavering equilibrium and stepped out. It was like walking out of a darkened theater in the middle of the day. I held a hand up to shield my squinted eyes and surveyed my surroundings.

"Correct me if I am wrong, but shouldn't there be a building here?" I turned my gaze to Kacey as she emerged from the gangster mobile. "A shed or an outhouse? There's nothing here but a parking lot."

Kacey smiled. "I was saving this part as a surprise. You are going to love this. It's right over there. Just head for that sidewalk, past the trees. When you see the old locomotive, hang a right."

We did as Kacey instructed, heading for the edge of the lot. As we got closer, the front of an old steam locomotive began to reveal itself from behind the trees. A beautiful restoration set on display for ... and then I saw it. The entire landing had been hidden from view by the trees. It was a gondola. As my eyes followed the long cable hung with cable cars up the mountainside, I felt all the blood drain from my face, then my arms and my fingers, then everywhere else until I swore there wasn't a drop left in my entire body.

"You okay, Denise?" Kacey came up from behind me and touched my arm. I didn't even realize I had stopped. I put on my best smile and forced my feet to shuffle forward. "Yes. Just taking in the view."

"Isn't it great?" She beamed. "The entire resort is at the top of the mountain. You have to take this private gondola to get there. It's like the world's best lobby!" She looked at Angelo. "Each car holds ten people, and they get to take in this gorgeous view all the way up."

He smiled. "I love it."

"This is just for the guests, though," I interjected. "Too bad we can't ride it up."

"Of course, we can ride it up." Kacey bubbled with excitement. "They have it all ready for us." She pointed toward the gondola car at the platform. A man in a uniform stood by to assist us into the tub of hanging torture.

Angelo held out his arm. "What are we waiting for?"

Kacey wrapped her hand around his elbow, and they marched toward the open door of the gleaming death trap. I stared at the all glass enclosure, hanging from the spider thin cable, and couldn't make my legs move. I didn't have a problem with heights so much as that crunch that came with the hard landing at the bottom. I had to have a neighbor change my lightbulbs because I couldn't even stand on a chair. Lock me in a room with a month's worth of groceries on a high shelf, and I would starve to death right next to the ladder.

I closed my eyes and took a breath. Kacey could not beat me again. I was going to pick up my feet, get in that flying bubble coffin, and ride it all the way to a horrible, mangled death, even if it killed me.

Through sheer force of will, my right foot moved, then my left. I couldn't seem to take an adult sized step, so I resorted to speeding them up instead, doing a stiff, little penguin sprint to the finish line. As soon as I was inside, I wrapped both hands around the pole situated in the middle of the car, closed my eyes, and held on for dear life. The doors creaked shut with a rattled bang, and the car swept forward all at once, launching off the platform like a sling tossed egg.

"Are you sure you're all right?"

I opened my eyes to see Angelo and Kacey staring at me. Probably because I now hugged the center pole like a desperate stripper. I tried to let go and relax, but my hands wouldn't open, and I couldn't seem to straighten my arms. My breathing came in short, rapid-fire succession, and I could feel my pounding heartbeat in my head.

Angelo reached out for me, but it was like he was a million miles away. "Why don't you have a seat, Denise? We can have the gondola take us back down." I saw him turn to Kacey and ask something about calling someone. I couldn't hear what it was anymore. The pounding in my ears was so loud. Sweat dripped off my face, and the walls of the gondola darkened and began to close in. Panic gripped me tighter, and I heard a scream. Was that Kacey? The walls got closer, darker, until all I could see were my white knuckled fingers clasped around the pole. Then I heard my name one last time, far away, until even that disappeared into the darkness.

When I awoke, I was lying across the seat of Angelo's Cadillac, and Kacey sat next to me on the floor fanning me with her folder.

"I really think we should we call an ambulance." Her voice sounded shaken and unsure.

"She'll be fine." Angelo's voice now. "If she needs to go to the hospital, we'll take her. We don't need to embarrass her by surrounding the car with medics and police who will ask a bunch of questions."

I tried to sit up.

"Hold on a second." Kacey put a hand on my shoulder. "Go slow. What happened back there?"

As my senses came back to me, I realized what must have happened. Not only had Kacey one-upped me at every turn, I had just had a full-blown panic attack, complete with an unconscious meltdown. Ever the consummate professional, I did the only thing I could do. I leaned my head out the car door and threw up.

Kacey patted my back, offered me a napkin when I was through debasing myself, and handed me a little bottle of water. "Maybe we should get you home. Have you been feeling sick?"

I shook my head and took a sip of water, trying to formulate some sort of lie that would save what dignity I had left. "I felt fine. I'm not sure what happened. Last thing I remember we were walking to the gondola, then I was here. Did we go up to the retreat?"

I sat up and tried to put on a bewildered face. It wasn't hard. Bewildered wasn't far from half-drunk and humiliated.

"No." Kacey smoothed some of the hair out of my face and even did her best to fluff up the long locks here and there. "We called the gondola operator, and he got us down. Angelo's driver carried you here to the car."

Kacey reached over to a tissue box on the door, pulled one out and offered it to me. She made a subtle gesture toward her eyes, signaling the presence of mascara on my face. Probably about a gallon of it. I wiped away as much as I could and tried to pull myself together.

"Nothing like this has ever happened to me before." More

lies, but what the heck? Angelo probably thought I needed a psychiatrist at this point. "I must be dehydrated. Why don't you take Angelo up and show him around? I should probably stay here. I hope you don't mind."

I looked at Angelo, and he smiled at me. "I'm sure I am in good hands. My driver will get you anything you need while we're gone."

"Thank you." I tried not to look as humiliated as I felt. "I can take care of a few other details while you're up there."

I shifted my gaze to Kacey, who still wore a mask of concern. "Thanks." I meant it. For lots of things. Mostly because I could see that she knew what had really happened and had the good grace not to say it. "You two go. I'll be here when you get back."

Angelo got out first. As soon as he was out of earshot, Kacey leaned into me. "Don't worry. This is just between you and me."

As soon as she climbed out of the car, I felt the tears threaten to break down all my barriers. I had made such a mess of everything. The Kleenex in my hand looked like an old grease rag, thanks to all the mascara it had mopped off my face. I reached over to grab a fresh one to dab at my eyes. My purse was still in the car, so I pulled out the phone and called the only person I knew I could talk to. Rob's phone rang once, twice, four times, voice mail. Figured. I sent him a quick text on the off chance he might see it. I told him that a villainous gondola had chewed me up and spit me out in front of Kacey and a client. I waited. No response. There was no stopping the tears now. I pulled a handful of Kleenex out of the box and leaned back in the seat.

At least I would see him tonight. I could cry on his shoulder then. For now, I would have to be content crying in an antique limousine, wallowing in self-pity with a bottle of prohibition bourbon and Angelo's mafioso chauffeur.

CHAPTER SEVENTEEN

Rob and I sat next to each other on his living room couch, separating and boxing extra dishes, photos, linens—pretty much anything he didn't need for day-to-day living. He wanted to thin out and purge things he referred to as his *security anchors*. Stuff he used to remind himself how miserable he should be rather than getting on with his life. As painful as the process sounded, passing the time was easy as I recounted the day's disastrous events between Kacey, Angelo, and myself. Rob's reaction was less than sympathetic.

"I can't believe you tried to get on that thing." Rob wiped a tear out of his eye as he did his best to control his laughter. "Don't you remember what happened that time you, me, and Susan got on that glass elevator?"

I folded my arms and turned to level a deadpan glare in his direction.

"You tried to climb me like a jungle gym. You wrapped your arm around my neck so tight I thought you were going to kill me." He cackled again. "How did you get back to the car?"

I hesitated as Rob took a breath to maintain his composure.

"Apparently, his driver brought me back. I assume in some sort of very dignified fireman's carry or something."

I saw the impending eruption written all over Rob's face. He tried to hold it back, then burst out laughing. I couldn't help but join in, if nothing else because his laughter was so infectious.

"Come on." I reached out and smacked his chest. "It's not that funny." I let out a deep breath and thought about all the things I had screwed up today, this week, and how Kacey kept shining through it all.

I hung my head. "I've made a huge mess of this whole account." All my bottled-up emotions came rushing to the surface.

"That's not true." Rob put down the photo he'd been wrapping and pulled me into his arms. "It's okay."

I leaned my head against him and let the tears flow.

"Aww, come on. You haven't made a mess of anything. It sounds like Kacey has everything under control."

"That's the problem," I choked out. "She does have everything under control."

"What's wrong with that?"

"Because that should be me, not her." My voice went up an octave. "She's the new girl. I've been doing this forever."

"Oh, I see." He rubbed my back. "Well, even you are allowed to have an off day or two. You are not the patron saint of party planning you know."

I coughed out a little laugh. "Actually, I believe the jury's still out on that one."

Rob sat back and looked me in the eye. I stared back at him, trying to focus through my tears.

"You and I both know that company could not function without you. There's nothing to worry about. Take a breath, stop trying so hard, and trust your new assistant to get the job done. That's what she's there for. A resource to make your life easier, not a threat to make it worse."

He wiped the tears from my cheeks.

"You're better than this. No more feeling sorry for yourself and no more gondolas, glass elevators, or high-rise window washing. Not unless I am there with a camera to record the whole thing."

I narrowed my eyes at him. "You would?"

"Darn right. A video like that could win me thousands of dollars."

"You mean it would win me thousands of dollars," I said. "Don't forget you need my permission to use it."

He sighed. "All right. Fifty-fifty then."

I held out my hand, and we shook on the deal. "Not much chance of a photo op though. I don't ever plan on getting into one of those deathtraps again."

Rob chuckled.

"Except ..." I let out a deep breath. "Damn, I forgot. Kacey wants me to be at the party on Saturday. Will you come with me? I don't want to go alone, especially if I have to face that, that – thing again. I promise not to embarrass you—much. Besides, you clean up pretty good. Come on, I can't do it without you."

"Wow, how could I refuse with a compliment like that? I'll make sure my phone is charged." He grinned. "Wouldn't want to miss out on an opportunity to win all that cash."

I smacked his arm. "Not nice. I'm serious."

"I know, sorry." He put his hand on my leg. "Of course, I'll be there for you. Just tell me the time and place, and I'll be ready."

"Thanks. You're the best." I put my hand over his.

We went back to sorting and wrapping items. Rob broke the silence. "If it makes you feel any better, I had quite a day myself."

He recounted the trip he and Isaac took to the lookout tower and the reckless plunge he had made down the mountain. My hands went to my mouth in horror when he got to the end and described how close he almost came to driving right off the side of a cliff, never to be seen or heard of again.

"I don't know what I was thinking. These guys have slipped through my fingers so many times. I wanted them so bad, and I thought it might be my only chance. It was stupid."

I pulled my hand away from my face and punched him in the arm—hard.

"Ouch."

He reached up and rubbed the spot where I had hit him, but I found myself lashing out to hit him again. I must have pummeled his arm and shoulder half a dozen times before I could stop.

"Stupid? You're damn right it was stupid." I jabbed him one last time. "You could have died. You could have killed Isaac, and he has a family. What would I do if you weren't here? How could you be so selfish?"

He looked at me, stunned by my sudden fury.

"I'm sorry." He held up a hand, ready to ward off any more blows. "I just ... I don't know what got into me." He looked away and stared at the ground.

"I know you're still hurting, but that doesn't give you the right to be so reckless with your life. What happened to Susan wasn't your fault." I wiped the tears out of my own eyes and saw that they were beginning to form in Rob's. "I was there, remember? There was no way we could have known that snow would let go. She wanted the first crack at the run. It wasn't like any of us were inexperienced skiers, especially her."

I reached out and put a gentle hand on his cheek, turning his face toward mine. "Any one of us could have been caught in that avalanche. You, at least, gave her the best chance at survival. You found her when no one else could. You gave her those precious few days. The time to say goodbye."

My hand slipped from his cheek to his neck, but his sad, tortured eyes never left mine. "She wanted you to move on. Wanted us both to. Hard as it is to remember, her last words are ones I will cherish forever. She told us to be happy and live life.

You're a good man, Rob. The best man I know. You of all people should feel what it is to be happy again."

We sat there staring into one another's eyes for a moment, then almost as one—one thought, one movement—we leaned forward until our lips hovered just inches apart. We paused there, breathing each other in. The hesitation caused a moment of uncertainty. A pang of guilt, then our lips met in an eruption of pure emotion, and all doubt washed away. My skin felt as if it were on fire, and I could not seem to catch my breath. I held onto his strong neck, and he wove his hand into my hair, pulling me closer as the kiss became more intense.

When we parted, neither of us let go. We moved slow, drawing out the experience as if a simple kiss were something neither of us had ever fathomed in our wildest dreams. He wore the same intense expression of shock and bewilderment that I felt.

"I'm so sorry," he said, but his hand never left my shoulder, as if waiting for permission to kiss me again. Mine was on his too, lingering in expectation for what might happen next.

"Don't be." I smiled. "It was nice."

We stared at one another, and I felt him pull me toward him. Uncertainty rose in my chest again. This time like a battering ram, refusing to be ignored. This wasn't the right time. It needed to be different somehow. I let my hand slip to his chest and held him there. "Maybe I should go, before we rush into something we're not sure about."

Rob sat back and gave me a closed-lipped grin. He understood. Our friendship meant the world to both of us, and neither of us wanted to jeopardize that.

"I'll walk you to the door," he said. "Thanks for all your help tonight—about a lot of things."

We stood up, and I gathered my belongings and got ready to leave. We didn't say much. It was a little awkward, but I knew no matter what we would figure things out. When Rob opened the door for me, he put a hand on my arm. For a minute, I thought he might try to kiss me again, but he just looked at me instead.

"The other day you said something to me at Grumpy's. You said you didn't know what life would be like without me in it."

I looked down at the ground, remembering my unexpected comment.

"We got off on another subject that night, but I really wanted to tell you that I feel the same way. I don't know what my life would be without you in it either. I don't think I would have had the guts to say it though. Thanks for saying it to me."

I nodded. "Thanks back at ya."

He let go, and I headed out the door.

"See you tomorrow night at Grumpy's?" he called out.

"Wouldn't miss it." I waved and got into my car, wondering if anything would be the same between us ever again.

CHAPTER EIGHTEEN

Walking into the office the next morning felt like a whole new experience. I arrived an hour early as usual, and as usual, Kacey was there brewing coffee and organizing paperwork in blissful silence. Today, though, I didn't care. Rob had been right all along. She was hired to be my assistant; I should allow her to assist. The fact that she beat me here every morning was a good thing. This wasn't a competition. In fact, it should impress me that she was motivated enough to arrive in time to have everything ready before I got here. After all, was I any different?

My elevated mood probably had something to do with Rob too; although, I was almost afraid to be happy about it. Saying I had mixed feelings about the kiss he and I had shared was the understatement of the millennium. Susan had been my best friend, and Rob still mourned her death. Was it right for us to be together? It sure felt right last night. And what would we be risking? Rob was my best friend. Let's face it, my only real friend. What if our relationship went south? It wouldn't be like saying goodbye to some guy I had hooked up with. Life without Rob would be like life without chocolate—worse, life without air. My insides were doing cartwheels despite my brain's deepest reservations. I wanted to be happy but didn't know what I should do.

"Denise." Jim called out to me from his office. Apparently, he had taken to coming in early on a regular basis as well. He jumped up from behind his chair and hurried out to meet me at his door. "Get in here. How are you feeling? I know you consider a sick day sacrilege, but after yesterday, I figured even you would take the day off."

He guided me into his office and sat me down in one of his guest chairs and then leaned back on his desk. "Do you need anything?"

My mind had been so preoccupied with Rob it took a few seconds for me to switch gears. When I did, my motor redlined, and I leapt up to stand in front of him. "I can't believe this. Did Kacey scurry all the way to your house last night or just wait outside your office to tell you this morning?"

I opened and closed my fists, pumping them with anger. I looked out Jim's window to see if I could spot the lying little toadstool.

"Calm down." Jim reached out to grab one of my wrists, but I jerked it away. "Denise, Kacey didn't say anything to me."

"Yeah." I paced the small room. "You must have become psychic then. And I was just beginning to trust that little ..."

"Angelo called me at home last night." Jim raised his voice to cut me off mid-sentence. "He wanted to know how you were doing. He was genuinely concerned."

Jim stood and gestured for me to sit down again. Justified or not, my adrenaline-fueled anger took a moment to subside. When it did, I sat back down and tried to compose myself.

"I was going to tell you all about it this morning when I got in."

"No, you weren't." Jim laughed. "Give me a little credit. If you lost a leg, you would hop in here talking about the marathon you planned to run this afternoon."

He was right. I had no intention of telling him, but I didn't think I was as transparent as all that.

"Maybe so, but it was really nothing. I just had a little issue with ..." I struggled with whether to tell him the whole truth or not. "It was my stupid fear of heights. Kacey set up an event in Breckenridge for Angelo, and I made the uncalculated mistake of setting foot on the gondola of death."

Jim snorted and quickly reached up to cover his mouth.

"Go ahead, laugh. Rob just about had a seizure he thought it was so funny."

Jim moved his hand but couldn't quite mask his toothy grin. "How is Rob? I haven't seen him in quite a while."

"Other than offering hysterical laughter as comfort for my humiliation, he's good."

That broke him. Jim let out a wheezing laugh, and I joined him. At least my phobia was good for something.

"Look, the fact that you were even willing to get on that thing is just what I have been talking about." Jim quelled his laughter but still wore the smile. "You work too hard. Take on too much. I need you to slow down and pace yourself a little, so my star account winner is still with me when we grow this company into its own Fortune 500 slot."

I nodded and got ready to tell him I was ready to do just that, but he held up a hand before I had the chance.

"Don't *'I'm fine and you can handle it,'* or whatever else you were going to say."

I shook my head and tried to disagree, but he stood up and cut me off again.

"Not this time, Denise. You need a break. I decided to give the Angelo Scalari event to Kacey."

That hit me like a punch in the gut. My mouth hung open, and I felt all that adrenaline-fueled anger rev up for another lap.

"I reviewed her work, and she has done a great job. You can

guide her through any rough spots, but other than that, I want you to be hands off on this one."

Now I would be *her* assistant? Fat chance of that.

"If you think I am going to take a backseat to the biggest account this company has ever had, you're the one who has been working too hard." I stood up again, leaning in toward Jim as I punctuated each word with a finger pointed at his imported rug. "I have been here ten years. I can't believe you would even consider taking my account away and giving it to Kacey."

"I'm not taking it away." He said, not giving an inch. "The account is yours, but she will finish arranging the event. She is your assistant. Not your protégé. If I wanted someone to replace you, I would have hired someone with better credentials and more experience than her. And it would probably take two people, not one, so get over this insecurity complex and remind me why you are one of the top event planners in the state."

"And just how do you propose I do that?" I crossed my arms in defiance and stared him down. "Now that you *haven't* given my account to my *non-protégé* and all."

He raised his eyebrows and turned to circle around behind his desk again. "Funny you should ask. While you *aren't* working on the Angelo Scalari event, I do have something else I want you to do."

He offered me a gold embossed envelope. I stood there for a moment, staring at him with my arms crossed. When he didn't relent, I sighed and took it out if his hand.

"What's this? A birthday invitation?"

"Close. The Colorado Chamber of Commerce is holding its annual platinum member network gala. I want you to attend and do what you do best."

"And what's that?"

"Why are you making this so difficult?" Jim sighed. "I set you up with an assistant who works her ass off for you, now offer you an invitation to a swanky cocktail party, and all I get is grief."

That made me step back a little. He was right. Ungrateful wasn't just my middle name lately, it was my job description, title, and family crest.

"Is there anyone in particular I should look for?"

"That's the Denise I know and love." He smiled and nodded. "Their names and photos are in the envelope. Kacey is digging up their bios for you."

I turned to leave but stopped before I got to the door. "I'm sorry I have been so unappreciative. You're a great boss and a good friend. I just get a little ..."

"Crazy?"

"I was going to say passionate, but we can go with crazy."

Jim smiled. "Go straighten things out with Kacey. She's a good kid. All she wants to do is impress you. Reminds me of young planner I met years ago." He raised his eyebrows.

I smiled back at him then moved toward the door. "And I bet that planner is doing just fine on her own now." I winked at him.

"Denise..."

"I know, I know—go talk to Kacey," I said and closed his door.

CHAPTER NINETEEN

I expected Isaac's friend to meet us downtown at the vehicle maintenance shop. It was a huge complex full of government trucks, open work sheds, and grouchy mechanics, but Isaac's buddy made the trip to Golden to see us. I figured it might have something to do with the less than traditional techniques I planned to employ in my investigation and the fact that I was asking him to alter government equipment to do it. Either way, I was grateful for his help and equally as grateful that I didn't have to fight midday traffic.

The short trip to Isaac's office did give me some time to think about Denise's visit the previous evening. I never thought a ten second action could fill me with so many conflicting emotions. I hadn't planned to kiss her, but it felt right, at least at the time. Now ... I couldn't help but wonder what was on her mind. Was she happy? Glad? Did she regret it? Part of me dreaded the thought of even talking about it. The last thing I wanted to do was jeopardize our friendship. But suddenly, I wasn't sure if friendship was enough.

I was careful to pack up all my emotional baggage before I pulled into the parking lot of the ranger station. The last thing I needed was Isaac needling me about my night with Denise. Airing my relationship issues during a special trailer park episode of Jerry Springer would be less painful. A vehicle caught my attention as I parked. A seventy-something Chevy truck with a home sprayed camo job. Just the type of truck I dreaded seeing out the woods. It screamed come find me, I'm up to no good.

I got out of my jeep and headed for the entrance of the station, but before I made it to the doors, a tree-trunk of a man burst out onto the walkway and shouldered me to the side. He was burly, bald, and had a black beard wild enough to make a pirate jealous. Bluing tribal tattoos colored his tanned skin, even on his neck and scalp, and his eyes were weighed down by dark bags that carried more fury than exhaustion. He wore a thick, gold ring in his left ear that completed the buccaneer motif, making him look like a shipwrecked sailor who had never found his way back to the sea.

Momentary anger threated to override my mouth and offer a disrespectful greeting, but I got it under control and turned to watch him go instead. I knew better than to turn my back on someone willing to bull through a stranger the way he had, especially considering I was in uniform. Better to watch him leave than offer a free target.

Isaac walked out the door just as the man jammed his camoed Chevy in gear and tore out of the lot.

"Another friendly tourist?" I kept my eye on the truck, watching it and the driver until they were both out of sight.

Isaac huffed. "That guy is a real piece of work. Been in here every day trying to get his snake back. He kept a Black Mamba as a pet, if you can believe that."

I raised my eyebrows. "Not exactly a fluffy kitten, but there's no law against owning one in this state—much as I disagree with it."

Isaac nodded. "True. But when we find Fluffy the Snake in his neighbor's bedroom, it tends to be a problem."

I grimaced.

"Twice," he added.

I couldn't help but laugh, hoping there wasn't a lethal end to the story.

"Fluffy must have liked his neighbor's cologne or something. The guy was lucky enough to spot it both times, but I figured twice was enough. Blackbeard isn't getting his pet snake back. He will just have to use a parrot like normal pirates."

I laughed out loud.

"Why don't you pull your Jeep behind the building? Jerry's waiting for us."

Isaac turned to head back in, but I put a hand on his shoulder to stop him.

"One sec. About that stunt I pulled yesterday." I took a step away and shoved my hands into my pockets trying to find the right words.

Isaac squared himself up to me and crossed his arms over his chest. He let me squirm for a few seconds then relaxed and jabbed me in the shoulder. "It's okay. I get it. You were in the moment."

I looked up and gave him a crooked smile, but his face turned serious.

"That's not to say what you did wasn't stupid. I want to know when you go after these guys, you'll be smart. I don't want to be carrying your casket. You get me?"

I nodded. "From now on, my brain is running the show."

Isaac rolled his eyes and threw his hands into the air. "I said smart. Don't you listen to anything I say?"

I narrowed my eyes at him. "You're a regular comedian. Now can we go meet your friend?"

Instead of heading for the building, Isaac went to the passenger side of my Jeep. "I guess you can give me a ride there as long as you keep us in one piece. No Dukes of Hazzard stunts."

I walked over to my side and crawled behind the wheel.

"What if we have to jump a ravine to get there? Bo Duke never missed."

"I see you as more of a Daisy Duke. You do have the Jeep and all."

I glared at him as we backed up and rounded the building. "That was uncalled for—and you just named my jeep."

Isaac laughed and pointed to a panel truck parked at the rear of the building. "Jerry's right over there."

I pulled in beside it, and we were met by a jolly-looking man wearing thick glasses, a plaid shirt, and wide suspenders. His thin, graying hair was windswept in every direction.

Jerry waved at us with stubby fingers, and I could tell by his smile that I was going to like him.

Isaac was already standing next to him when I got around to their side of the Jeep. "Rob, this is Jerry. Jerry, my friend Rob."

Jerry held out his hand, and I shook it. His grip felt rough and tough as iron. "So, I hear you need to track down some frequency bandits."

I nodded. "Isaac said you're the best in the business."

Jerry shrugged and walked to the back of his truck. "More of a hobby really, but I have never run up against a fox hunt that could beat me."

He pulled out what looked like a portable radio attached to a three-foot metal antenna shaped like a flat Christmas tree.

"I think this will get you where you're going, once you're close. You will have to rotate the end of this antenna around until you see the indicator light up in the radio's screen. When it does, head in that direction."

"Easy enough." I took the contraption out of his hands and tested the balance. It was awkward, but it wasn't heavy. It would be simple enough to use out in the field.

"You said when I get close." I set the whole thing down in the tailgate of his truck. "What sort of range will it have?"

"The handheld unit will have to be within a quarter mile—maybe less when you get into the trees."

Jerry opened another compartment on the side of his truck and pulled out a much larger unit designed to be mounted inside a vehicle. "This is one is better. It has a fifty-mile range—sometimes more if you get up high on a pass. I'll mount a directional antenna array on the top of your Jeep, and you'll be a gas guzzling bloodhound. Just follow the arrows on the screen." Jerry held up something that resembled a small tablet. "This will give you a heading and signal strength. When the meter on the side gets close to the top, you are close to your bandits. You can get out and use your portable to run them down the rest of the way, if you have to. Or if you're lucky, just pull up next to their minivan and bust 'em."

I laughed. "If it is that easy, I'll be back to buy you both steak dinners."

"You got a deal. Now give me a couple of hours with your little beauty, and I'll have you up and ready for business."

I reached out and shook Jerry's hand again. I knew even with his equipment, finding my poachers would be like trolling the ocean with a butterfly net, but it was better than trolling with no net at all.

My phone buzzed in my pocket, and I excused myself to check and see who had sent me a message. It turned out to be Denise.

Sorry, I have to flake out on Grumpy's tonight. Working late.

I stared at the message for a moment. My face began to pinch in anger, then uncertainty and frustration. I went to type in a reply, but everything I said seemed terse or childish, so I wound up erasing and starting over again several times. Why was I so angry? Denise had called off lots of times. This felt more like ... jealousy.

I knew she was probably staring at her phone, waiting for me to respond so I typed, *Sounds good. Since when are you on the late shift?*

I hit send and re-read my message, cursing even that snide remark. My phone remained quiet for a moment, then the three flashing dots told me she was typing a response. I realized I was holding my breath and forced myself to breathe. This was so stupid. This was Denise. We'd known each other forever. We met or talked almost every day. Why was a simple text message tying me into knots?

Even as I thought it, I knew why. The kiss. Susan. I felt like I was betraying my wife with her best friend. But was I?

My phone buzzed again.

Working late to beat the new girl. Tell you all about it tomorrow.

I sighed. Whatever was going on in my head, I needed to figure it out. Susan had been the very air I breathed, but she was gone. And I still had to find a way to live. Come what may, Denise was here, and so was I. Maybe it was time to see if there was something more than friendship hiding beneath the surface of all this grief.

I typed a response, hesitated, erased it, typed it again, closed my eyes, and hit send.

It's a date!

CHAPTER TWENTY

*I*t's a date!

I grinned at Rob's message when I rounded the corner to my cubicle to see Kacey sitting next to my desk. As soon as I came into view, she bounced up, wringing her hands in front of her chest, spouting apologies and explanations like a professional auctioneer.

"Denise, I am so sorry. I want you to know I didn't ask to be put on Angelo's account. I told Jim I wouldn't do it, but he said I was hired to help you and that's what you needed right now whether you realized it or not. I said I still thought it was wrong, and he said if I couldn't handle the job, he would find someone who could." Tears began to flow out of Kacey's eyes, and her face started to scrunch up as if a little gnome were inside her head squishing everything together. "I really love working with you, and I don't want to lose my job. I'm trying so hard, and I feel like I keep screwing everything up, and now you are mad at me —"

I sighed and pulled her in for a hug. "All right. Stop that. I'm not mad at you. At least, I'm not mad at you anymore. Geez, how could anyone be mad after an apology like that?"

Kacey coughed out a laugh and stepped back. I let go of everything but her hand and then noticed her outfit for the first time. Navy pinstriped pantsuit with a powder blue blouse and black heels. It was a mirror image to mine—well almost. Her blouse was nicer, the suit appeared to be high end, and her shoes had enough style to make my plain pumps want to hide in the closet from shame. The girl even dressed better than I did when we wore the same thing.

She saw me eying her outfit and covered her face with her free hand. "Great. I can't even get this right."

She tried to pull her other hand away, but I held on, forcing her to look back up at me. "Don't worry about it. I'll change later. I always keep a spare outfit at the office." As I said it, I remembered that my spare clothes had already been used, also thanks to Kacey, and I hadn't had time to replace them yet. I decided not to air this out loud, as my solution seemed to make Kacey feel better.

"You always seem to know what to do."

I grabbed a couple of tissues off my desk and handed them to her so she could dab the makeup out from under her eyes.

"Comes with the territory, I guess. For now, get yourself cleaned up, and let's figure out what else you need to do for this event."

I thought she was going to start crying again, but she held it together and forced a smile. "Thanks, Denise. I really am sorry if it feels like I am barging in on your territory."

"It does, and you are, but that's okay. We'll figure it out."

She pulled me into another hug before I could stop her.

"Okay," I said. "We're good. Catch me up on where you are for the event."

I sat down at my desk, and she followed suit, picking up a folder with one hand as she dabbed at her face with the other. "I did quite a bit of digging on Angelo and his company. It looks like he runs an incredibly successful tourism business. He has clients all over the world and offers immersive adventures in places like India, Africa, the Galapagos." She flipped out a sheet of paper riddled with bullet points and offered it to me. I took it and laid the sheet on my desk where I could follow along. "He's even opened up an American tour for people who want to experience places like Yosemite and the Rocky Mountains. I connected with an outdoor outfitter, and they are willing to let me raid their warehouse for décor. I was thinking ..."

I continued to stare at Kacey's ultra-organized talking paper but seeing the writing on the page somehow brought me back to Rob's text. I hadn't even responded to him. I wondered how serious he was about that last comment. Did he mean he wanted us to go on a real date? What if I was reading more into that kiss than there really was? What if there really *was* more to that kiss? Thinking about him, his warm lips on mine, his strong arms around me, sent a surge of tingles through my body. My life was a mess. I was a mess. Rob needed someone stable. Someone who wasn't ... well, me—right? Rob was such a good guy. I, on the other hand, had issues...

"What's wrong? What did I do? I knew I would screw something up."

Kacey put a hand on her forehead and scrutinized her list while I came back to reality. I realized my worry and concern over my life had knitted my features into an expression of pure terror. It must have looked like I had seen or heard something terrible in her placid presentation.

"Yes," I stammered. "I mean no, there is nothing wrong. Everything looks great, and yes, I am listening."

I sat up and handed the paper back to Kacey, essentially cutting off the remainder of her presentation.

"Look. Here's all you need to know about Angelo. He has more money than he knows what to do with. Anything you do, make it bigger, better, and more extravagant than you or anyone else has ever heard of before. Do not look for ways to cut costs. It worked out with your uncle, but you didn't have to sacrifice the product for price. Do you follow my meaning?"

Kacey beamed. You would think she had just scaled a Tibetan Mountain seeking wisdom, and I was the long-lost Dalai Lama. Every word I uttered was priceless, and she gathered them like precious stones, putting them in her mental lockbox for safekeeping. It was an uncomfortable moment, right up there with the time I accidentally tucked the back of my skirt into my pantyhose. I had shared way too much of myself at the Colorado Tourism brunch that day.

Kacey nodded and stood up. "I got it. Thank you so much, Denise."

I gave her a crooked smile. "Don't mention it. If you run into any trouble let me know. Number one rule is keep the client happy. Remember that, and you'll be fine."

Kacey tore a pen out of her pocket and scrawled the words across the front of her file folder as if she might forget the epiphany if she didn't write it down.

"Okay, I will. Thanks again."

She started to leave, then turned back, shuffling the stack of folders in her hands. "I almost forgot. Jim asked me to get you some information. A couple of guys you're meeting tonight at the event, I guess?"

She offered me two folders out of the pile. "I didn't really get a chance to review them. If you want me to, I can read through them and —"

I snatched them out of her hands and tucked both folders under my arm. "No, thanks. I have this covered."

Kacey hesitated a moment, but when I didn't offer anything but a friendly smile, she turned to head back toward her desk.

I sank back down in my chair and plopped the files onto my

desk. Jim was right. Tonight was just what I needed. An evening in my element, networking with new clients, unmolested by Kacey's glittery voodoo. I could redeem myself and recharge my own mojo. Maybe the extra time would help me figure out what to do about Rob too.

CHAPTER TWENTY-ONE

I smoothed out my dress, straightened my spine, and strolled into The Denver Chamber of Commerce like I owned the place. They always pulled out all the stops for these elite member mixers. This party was no different. The booze was top shelf, the food gourmet, and the wait staff looked more over the top than a diamond Rolex. If I weren't so good at my job, I'd be a little jealous. A quick scan over the few dozen people already there landed me on one of my targets.

"Brett Hamilton." A tall, late twenties-ish man with thick, black hair spun around at the mention of his name. He was going for confident and casual, with an open suit jacket and loose tie. His beer swayed where he held it by the neck, and he smiled.

"At your service. To what do I owe the pleasure of this meeting?"

The two men he had been talking to, and now consequently ignored, stared at me as well. They were less than amused by my sudden intrusion.

I held out a hand. "I'm Denise Baldwin, with Platinum Events. I didn't mean to interrupt. I just wanted to introduce myself."

He shook my hand. "Well, count yourself introduced,

Denise." He stepped aside and motioned to the men standing behind him. "These are my accountants. They were just boring me with lots of numbers and talk about money. Let's pretend they're not here and walk away. I don't think they'll notice."

They held fast to their deadpan expressions. My laugh that followed did not help. Brett must have taken this as an agreement to his plan because he waved to no one, as if he had just been hailed from across the room and grabbed my hand to head off at a determined pace.

He wove us through the din of chatting people enjoying their cocktails and fancy hors d'oeuvres. Brett didn't stop until we stood on the other side of the room. I couldn't help but steal a glance at his accountants. We hadn't escaped their view, not by a long shot. They just shook their heads and turned away as if this were an everyday occurrence.

"I don't know if it's a good idea to make your accountants mad." I pulled my hand away from his and reached for a glass of wine on a passing drink tray. "They handle all your money, you know."

Brett shrugged. "True, but they won't do anything with it. Not maliciously anyway. Accountants understand numbers and dollar signs. They have no imagination. They could sign an order to turn my uptown office into a giant pig farm, and no one would notice until it was too late, but they won't. Stealing money is the most creative thing they come up with, and that's so cliché. Accountants skimming off the top? It's been done."

I laughed again. "I guess I see your point."

Brett took another swig of his beer and nodded at me. "So, tell me about you. How do you know me? And where did you get that dress?"

He took a step back and looked me over. I had gone home to don my swankiest black dress. I only broke it out for special occasions. After the week I had, I decided to come in with the big guns.

"Glad you like it. Haven't worn it in years." I spun around, holding my wineglass high in the air. "I almost forgot this old thing was hanging in the closet."

"Well, I'm sure I speak for everyone here when I say thank the good cheeses of Wisconsin that you found it. Denise, was it?"

"Yes," I said. "With Platinum Events. We organize events that make this one look like a garage sale."

Brett coughed out a laugh. "Pretty big claim. Why don't I go get us some fresh drinks, and you can tell me all about it?"

I downed the rest of my wine in one gulp and handed him my empty glass. "I think that sounds lovely."

Brett hurried off toward the bar, and I took the opportunity to survey the room for more prospective clients. The venue impressed me, despite my garage sale comment. The Denver Chamber of Commerce was located right off Market Street and hosted the event to showcase their amazing renovations. They managed to mix rustic wood styling with a state-of-the-art feel. They had plenty of space and the clientele to fill it. If I were ever to work somewhere else, this would be on my short list.

I admired the artwork of a buffalo photographed in mid-winter when someone tapped my shoulder from behind. I expected to see Brett, with fresh libations and a mouth full of suave compliments, but instead I found myself face-to-face with a tall, attractive gentleman with salt and pepper hair. His well-tailored look opposed Brett's unbuttoned swagger in every way that mattered.

"I hope I'm not bothering you, but are you Denise Baldwin?"

I smiled. "The very same."

I couldn't believe my luck. The two people I had come to meet, and I ran into both of them within minutes of one another. "And you are Frank Landen. You run one of the largest not-for-profit organizations in the country."

He nodded and bowed his head. "Your reputation precedes

you as well. I've heard you have a talent for organizing fantastic events. We could use talent like that to attract contributors."

"You're making this too easy for me." I laughed. "I'm supposed to be the one talking you into working with us."

Frank grinned and turned as if he were going to walk away. "I could make a run for it, if that would make you feel better."

"It might," I said. "But I would never catch you in these heels. I guess you'll have to stay."

He shrugged in concession and faced me again. "Well, the offer's still on the table, if you change your mind."

I glanced over his shoulder and scanned the room wondering where Brett had gotten off to. Much as I was enjoying Frank's company, I didn't want to let my first fish off the line just yet.

"I would love to get together with you sometime," I said, turning my attention to Frank again. "We could talk about what type of events you're looking for, how we could impress your contributors, and discuss what we can provide."

My eyes had just flitted back to his when I spotted Brett lounging at the bar. When I glanced over again, my head pounded with rage.

"Are you all right?"

I jerked my head toward Frank, realizing I had blanked him out completely. My free hand had balled into a fist, and my jaw clenched so tight my teeth hurt.

I forced myself to take a deep breath and relax. "Yes, I'm fine. Sorry. I just recognized someone over there, that's all."

"Well, I pity the poor soul, whoever they are." He laughed.

I forced a grin and pulled a card out of my clutch. "Shall we get together next week? I'm free on Monday."

"Monday is perfect." He took my card and offered me one of his from his inside jacket pocket. "I'll come to your office. Shall we say nine o'clock?"

"Nine it is." I flashed him my best smile while I shook his

hand. "It was a pleasure meeting you, Frank. I look forward to seeing you again on Monday."

He nodded. "Good luck with your—friend."

I turned my gaze to where Brett was sitting. He let out a laugh that carried all the way across the room and patted the shoulder of a cute, little redhead wearing a pinstriped business suit and a powder blue blouse. I didn't know what Kacey was up to, but I was about to find out.

CHAPTER TWENTY-TWO

"What brings you all the way out here tonight?" Kacey blanched the moment she heard my voice. She had been in the process of telling some sort of story but cut it off mid-sentence when I strolled up. "I thought you were working on that big account."

"Jim told me to cut out early and meet you here." Her eyes pleaded with me to understand. "I think he wanted me to shadow you and see how ..."

Her gaze flicked from me to Brett and back again.

I was not about to offer her a way out of this particular corner. I stood there and laid a hand on Brett's shoulder, letting my head tilt to the side a little in feigned confusion.

Seconds clicked by, and tiny balls of sweat beaded on Kacey's forehead. The torture went on not nearly long enough before Brett coughed out a laugh and slapped the top of the bar. "We're just giving you a hard time. This is a meet and greet. Your boss wanted you to come down and see how a pro works the room. Am I right, Denise?" He looked at me and raised his eyebrows.

Kacey heaved out a small laugh and turned her eyes to the floor. She appeared so relieved you would have thought he told her she was no longer responsible for flipping the switch at the state execution.

"Speaking of working a room," I turned my attention to Brett again. "You never came back with my drink."

"So true." He pressed the palms of his hands together and made a show of bowing in my direction. "Can you ever forgive me?"

"That depends."

"On?" He raised an eyebrow but kept his hands in place.

"On whether or not I get a drink in the next sixty seconds."

Brett spun to the bar and yelled. "Barkeep. I need a bottle of wine and three glasses, immediately."

I could not help but notice the odd number he requested and cringed a little inside. There was no way Kacey would upstage me tonight. Not here, not now. I was on my game, and she had stepped in too far, whether Jim sent her down or not.

"Why don't we go to the balcony?" I pointed to the big glass doors on the far side of the room. "They have the heaters going, and we can have a little privacy next to the fire."

I shot him a grin playful enough to make him regret inviting Kacey to our private soiree. He glanced toward the doors, and his gaze went to Kacey, then back to me. That's right. Three's a crowd.

"All right," he said. "Let's all go out and get some air."

Curses.

"Why don't you two go on out?" Kacey said. "I'll get the wine and be right behind you."

Curses twice. "Thanks, Kacey. You're a doll." I snaked my arm into Brett's, and together we meandered through the crowd to the balcony.

The initial blast of brisk winter air caused me to grip his arm tighter. Towering heaters, glowing orange spires with bright blue flames, stood between wrought iron tables, and in the center, a fire pit roared. Cushioned outdoor seating surrounded the flickering centerpiece and was cozy enough to be a honeymoon destination. We could even see the night-lively street, one level down, over the rail.

Brett led me to one of the comfy-looking couches facing the fire, and I sat down. He seated himself beside me, and as soon as he did, I scooted in closer. "A bit chilly out here, don't you think?"

It wasn't in the least, not with all these pyres roaring around us, but I was not about to let Kacey get the upper hand. "So, tell me more about what you do. I read a little about you and one article said you are a self-made man."

He laughed at that, and so did I. "Self-made, bought, and paid for. I saw a market and took advantage of it. That's what people like you and I do right?" He lifted his arm and laid it across the top of the couch behind me. "Capitalize on a situation when it presents itself?"

I tittered out a laugh, but this time it was harder to make it sound genuine.

"Did someone out here order a bottle of wine?"

Kacey sauntered out with a tray topped with an expensive looking red and three glasses. Brett jumped up as she approached and took it from her, setting the whole thing down on a small end table. The bottle glugged as he poured us three healthy glasses. Kacey was about to sit next to me, but I reached across the couch, blocking her parking spot with my body as I grabbed my glass.

"This looks great. Thanks, Kacey."

She took the hint and scooted around to another couch, perching on the edge like a bird.

Brett swung around and offered her a glass, then took his place next to me again.

"You were just about to tell me about what you do," I said steering the conversation back to Brett. "Something about being bought and paid for?"

I shot him a playful wink, and he grinned, shaking his head. "That's not exactly what I said."

I laughed. "Close enough. So, tell me. What was this amazing opportunity you took advantage of?"

I draped my hand onto his shoulder, and his grin deepened. Kacey saw this and looked away, as if she were seeing something she shouldn't. If you come to play at the beach, don't get squeamish in the sand.

Brett pulled out his cell phone. "I created the Personal Paparazzi, a drone that follows you and photographs events automatically." He pointed into the air, and I looked up to see a drone descend out of the sky. It was so quiet I could hardly hear it.

"My little companion knows where I am and takes pictures of me and my friends on trips, at parties, whatever. It's quiet, pairs with any cellphone, and has a flight time of eight hours."

I gawked at the hovering craft. "You're kidding. Is it taking pictures of us right now?"

Brett nodded and raised his glass to the craft. "I just told it to run a bunch of the three of us."

Time to go for broke. I stood up and threw myself across Brett's lap and hooked an arm around his neck, posing for the camera with my wineglass. I was feeling every drop of alcohol I'd had that evening, and my poses showed it. I stuck my leg out, leaned back, made faces. I made sure he would have a whole scrapbook of photos to remember me by.

Before the shoot was over, Kacey stood, escaping our lurid movements. "It's getting late. I think I should be going."

"Late?" I gulped another swig of wine. "Well, that's how this younger generation is. They just don't know how to have fun."

I stood too, then so did Brett. I thought he might try and follow her toward the doors, so I wrapped my arms around his elbow, and we stumbled into the balcony's railing together.

"Have a good night, Kacey." I waved at her. I was feeling more and more like I should be sitting down. "I'll see you bright and early tomorrow."

I laughed, even though I wasn't sure why. Brett turned and I found myself leaning in toward him. "I guess it's just the two of us." My words were a little slurred, but I was pretty sure they all came out in the right order.

"Denise?"

The familiar voice came from below. A dark figure on the street peered up at me. I squinted to make out his face, then he called out again, and I didn't have to wonder anymore.

"It's Rob. What are you doing up there?"

CHAPTER TWENTY-THREE

"Rob, is that you?" All of a sudden, my proximity to Brett felt very uncomfortable.

"I just told you it was," he answered. "What are you doing up there? I thought you had to work late tonight."

I tried to make my sudden retreat from Brett look natural, but I was pretty sure it looked more like I was scraping something gooey off my hip. "I *am* working."

I spotted Kacey walking on the street near Rob and called out to her, hoping to avert our conversation for a moment.

"Kacey. Have you met my friend, Rob? No, of course you haven't. What am I saying? Rob, Kacey—Kacey, Rob."

She looked up at me and eyed the stranger standing on the street with suspicion.

"I've heard a lot about you, Kacey." Rob stepped forward to shake her hand, and she reciprocated in kind. "It's nice to finally meet you."

Kacey looked up at me, squinting into the overhead lights. "I wish I could say the same. Are you one of her ..." she hesitated, "clients?"

Her tone implied the word, client, had a meaning other than business associate.

Rob let go of Kacey's hand and looked up at me again. The weight of his gaze made me want to step away from the edge and hide. Why was I feeling so guilty? I had a right to have a good time. Just because Kacey couldn't keep up with a pro like me, that wasn't my fault.

As I stared down at the two of them, a wave of sickening shame washed over me. Had I really sunk this low? Some kind of pro I turned out to be. Kacey came here to learn, to assist, and be mentored, and here I am, all but selling my body just to get a client. I don't know if I had ever been quite this disgusted with myself.

"Denise? Are you all right?" Rob asked.

Check that. Now was definitely the worst. Not only had I humiliated myself in front of our firm's new recruit and a potential client, I could now add Rob to the list.

"I'm fine." I waved. "What are you doing downtown? You're not usually part of the nightlife crowd."

Rob's gaze shifted between me and Brett. I tried to look casual as I leaned against the rail and pretended not to notice. To Brett's credit, he just stood there, sipping his wine and watching our conversation.

"Lost a bet. Isaac made me take him to the Cheesecake Factory after work. I swear his wife must feed him seaweed and tofu at home because all he wants to do with me is eat."

I laughed. It was a comfortable feeling, and all of a sudden, I would have given about anything to be standing down on the street with him rather than up on the balcony with tall, rumpled, and leering.

Brett took the wine glass from my hand.

"Well, I better go." Rob nodded at Kacey. "It was nice to meet you."

She smiled at him but didn't look up at me. Instead, she just headed off in the other direction as if she were too embarrassed to peek up at us again. I almost wished Rob would do the same.

"You and your friend have fun." He motioned toward Brett. "I'll catch you later."

"Tomorrow night." I blurted it out a little too fast, stealing a sideling glance at Brett. Why did I care if he noticed anyway? "Same place, same time."

Rob waved but didn't say anything else. He just disappeared into the mix of lights, people, and traffic.

I watched him for as long as I could. When I couldn't see him anymore, I felt an overwhelming urge to run down the stairs and go after him. I looked down, thinking I would try, when Brett held out my wine glass, refreshed with a hefty compliment of wine.

"Where were we?"

I painted on a smile and took the glass out of his hand when he didn't relent. Brett now looked like nothing more than a guy doing his best to get into my pants, which of course was exactly where I was leading him five minutes ago. I cringed to think it may have worked had Rob not come along to knock me off my self-righteous high horse.

"I think I'm going to head out too." I leaned over to set my glass on the table next to me, but Brett closed in, cutting me off.

"You can't leave now. We were just starting to have fun."

He pressed in close, trapping me up against the rail. I looked around for a way out but realized we were the only ones out here. My slut act had probably driven more than just Kacey off. Great. Where was a knight in shining armor when a damsel needed one? Oh yeah, I drove him off too.

"I'm sorry if I gave you the wrong idea, but —"

"Don't you worry." Brett leaned in closer, interrupting me. "I have lots of ideas."

I put my hand on his chest and tried to push him back. "Look, I probably took things a little too far. But I'm telling you now, this needs to stop."

He grinned and didn't budge. "Stop? We're just getting started."

I felt something slip in behind me and down my thigh. A cold hand and uninvited fingers. Enough was enough. Creepy flirting was one thing. Groping ...

I brought my knee up hard between his legs, and Brett let out a mouse-sized squeak before he doubled over and backed away.

I shoved him onto the couch and picked up the glass on the table. "I hate to see good wine go to waste." I poured the entire contents over his head. He held his crotch and tried to wheeze out some sort of response, but I didn't stay long enough to hear what it was. Lucky for him, and me, there was no one on the balcony to witness that either. Without another word, I strolled over to the balcony doors, made my way through the thinning crowd inside, and headed to the exit.

CHAPTER TWENTY-FOUR

I yanked on the wrench connected to the antenna array on my Jeep. Jerry, Isaac's frequency tracker friend, had showed me how to adjust it. He hadn't told me the process would involve endless roadside trial and error micromovements that would drive a swiss watch repairman mad.

My wrench slipped for the umpteenth time, and I reared back to smash the entire thing Hulk-style. The Bruce Banner in me took over before I did though. It wasn't the antenna array, or the tracker, or even the fact that I had spent the entire day circling the forests without a single blip, beep, or go-screw-yourself from the tracking display on my dash. It was Denise.

Last night had dug so deep under my skin I couldn't sleep. Moreover, I didn't even know why. Denise had no commitment to me. She could do anything she liked and always had. I knew about her bar exploits and her not-so-serious affairs. She had always played the field and had fun doing it. So why had yesterday gotten to me so much?

When I saw her hanging all over that guy, I had wanted to climb the wall and pull him over the edge. I hadn't felt that kind of jealousy since ... well, maybe never. Even Susan hadn't brought out that kind of anger in me. Was it lust? Passion? Something more than that? Whatever it was, it drove me nuts.

I looped my wrench around the adjustment bar on the antenna array as a motor home passed by, whipping wind into my face, and tightened it down one last time.

This needed to stop. Denise had her own life to live, and I had no right to expect any different. I climbed down, opened the passenger door to my Jeep, and leaned against the frame, staring at the blank display screen.

Then again, why couldn't I expect something different? Maybe Denise was ready for a change. For that matter, maybe I was too.

Images of her hanging on that stranger barged into my thoughts again, pushing the maybes and what ifs away. She had been all over him, and he soaked in every bit of it. Who could blame him? Denise was a beautiful woman. More than beautiful. She was smart, funny, caring—not that the dark-haired loser would care about any of that. He would only be after one thing.

I threw my wrench onto the floorboard with a clang and slammed the door.

And what was with that comment Kacey made? Denise had never even mentioned me before? Thanks a lot. At least she seemed to be as disgusted with their little show as I had. I suddenly felt more than a little empathy for Kacey.

I pulled out my phone and checked the messages again. I was too deep into the mountains to get much service, but text messages would get through—eventually. The least Denise could do was say ... what would she say?

Had a great time last night. Wish you were there!

Whatever. It was time to pack up and head down the hill anyway. I needed to go meet Denise and settle all of this once and for all. At least then I wouldn't have to think about it anymore.

I stepped out into the empty road and opened my driver's door to swing a leg inside, then I froze.

Had I just heard something? I couldn't be sure with all the noise I made stepping into the vehicle.

I stood still as a statue, one hand and one leg inside the cab, then I heard it again. A single beep. This time I saw the directional arrow light up on my antennae display. I could hardly believe it. I had a hit. I climbed into the cab and started the engine, abandoning any thought of Grumpy's Happy Shack.

I grabbed the handset to my radio and keyed the mic.

"Base 3, this is Patrol 6."

I let go and heard nothing but static.

"Base 3, this is Patrol 6, respond."

Still nothing. So much for calling Isaac for backup.

I pulled out my cell phone and tried a text.

Got a hit. Going to try and run them down. No radio. Msg me if you receive!

I hit send only to have it bounce back as *unable to send*. Great. I would just have to hope it would find its way out to Isaac sooner or later.

I got ready to take off and paused. Frustrated or not, I wouldn't leave Denise hanging.

I scrawled one more hasty message, then tossed the phone on my seat. All I could do was hope it found a signal while I tracked down my drone flying poachers.

CHAPTER TWENTY-FIVE

"Where's the superhero this evening?"

I looked up from our usual table and shrugged at Al. He sported a blue Hawaiian shirt today. Must have been feeling a little somber when he got up. Join the club.

"I think he's running late. I saw him last night. He said he would be here."

Al nodded and appraised the other patrons in the bar the way a hardened field commander might survey the enemy before a battle. Instead of walking away, he just stood there, drying the inside of a high-ball glass in silence.

I waited a few moments until it was too awkward to bear anymore. "Do you need something or have a question?"

He looked down his nose at me and raised an eyebrow.

"Sorry, I didn't mean it like that. I guess I'm a little on edge."

"Happy to listen if you want to air it out. Can't guarantee I'll care, but as long as nothing more interesting happens, I'll lend an ear."

I chuckled and took a sip of my Coke. I decided I'd had enough liquor last night to last me a couple of millennia. "I guess I'm questioning if I've made the best choices lately."

"That's easy. Have you seen the guys you take home?"

"Thanks a lot."

Al nodded, unfazed.

"It's not just that." I twisted a napkin in my fingers. "My career has always been my top priority. All that relationship mess, I never wanted anything to do with it—at least I thought I didn't."

"Funny thing about love —"

"Whoa." I looked at him. "No one said anything about love. We're talking about life choices."

Al stopped toweling his glass and glared at me with his angry, bulging eyes until I wanted to sink under the table and cry for mercy. "Sorry, please go on."

"As I was saying," he resumed his glass buffing and continued to appraise the room with his combat stare. "Funny thing about love is, it always shows up when you least expect it. You can hunt love down, try to kill it and hang it on your mantle all glittered up with pink pixie dust, but love will never work out until it wanders in and craps all over your carpet on its own."

I blinked at him. "I have never been so appalled and impressed at the same time."

"I get that a lot. Usually in the bedroom."

I sputtered out a laugh. He gave me the smallest of smiles before he spun around and left.

"Thanks, Al!" I said after him.

He raised his hand and headed off with a drink menu to terrorize a couple of newbies.

Love. I was not in love. Not like that anyway. Rob and I had known each other forever. I loved him like a ... not a brother exactly, for some reason that seemed wrong. Even that realization sent my head spinning. What is going on with me that I couldn't even keep my life straight? I had lost control of one of the biggest accounts I've ever had. Kacey probably thinks I'm some sort of hooker, and now Rob's mad at me. Which he doesn't even have a right to be. I do what I want, when I want.

So why did I feel so guilty about everything I had done lately?

I put my head down on the table and groaned. Picking up a cute guy didn't even sound fun anymore. I really was sick.

My phone buzzed, so I straightened and pulled it out of my pocket. A message from Rob. The moment I saw his name my heart began to pound. It felt like scratching off a winning lottery ticket, not a text message from a friend. What's wrong with me?

My turn to work late. Sorry. Have to catch you later.

As fast as my heart soared, it sank again. He was avoiding me. That's all there was to it. I tried to respond, but nothing came back. It didn't even show that my message had been read. How many times had I given other people the cold shoulder? Now I was on the receiving end. And from my best friend. I stared at the phone, willing it to show a response. Instead the screen went dark, matching my mood.

I tossed my phone into my purse. I couldn't believe he wasn't man enough to come here and face me. Be mad at me, fine. Tell me I'm a horrible person, whatever, but come and do it to my face. Don't hide behind some lame excuse like having to work late.

Somewhere in the deep corners of my mind even I recognized the irony of my anger, but I didn't care. At least I wasn't sitting here feeling sorry for myself anymore. Now I was pissed. And I would rather be pissed than mopey any day.

If that's how he was going to be, then fine. I was perfectly happy enjoying the upcoming weekend by myself. Then it dawned on me. Tomorrow was Saturday. Not just any Saturday, but the day of Angelo's party. Kacey's big day. She had been out of the office today, and I was too wrapped up in my own drama to even realize why. I had thought she was just avoiding me because of the whole meet-and-greet debacle.

I sank into my chair and rested my head in my palms. Rob was supposed to be my date for the party, but now ... I wasn't sure what to do. My life was headed into a tailspin, and I didn't think it could get any worse. At the rate I was going, I had a pretty good idea it wouldn't be hard for me to find a way to get there.

CHAPTER TWENTY-SIX

I paused long enough to check my phone again. No signal. Not that there should be one. I wasn't on main street L.A. I was tromping through the forest in the middle of the Rockies. At some point, my messages to both Denise and Isaac had gone out, but I hadn't been smart enough to mention my location. Isaac didn't even have a general area to search. Unless a cellphone signal bounced down off a UFO, I was on my own. Even my radio returned nothing but static.

At least I had a clear sky above me, about an hour left of sunlight to see by, and it wasn't snowing. The only thing worse than wandering alone in the forest was wandering alone in the forest at night, especially in winter.

I slipped the phone in my pocket and hefted the handheld antenna connected to Jerry's portable tracking device. Testing the rig in an open parking lot was one thing. Slinging the receiver, battery pack, and giant antenna through the evergreens and underbrush was about as easy as swimming the English Channel wearing an Abrams Tank as a life preserver.

Good news was the signal was hot. Either these guys were

pumping out some serious power, or I was all but stomping in on top of them. My answer came a few seconds later.

A soft hum caught my attention, and I looked up to see a huge drone hovering overhead. The propellers were much larger than any of the homegrown jobs I had seen before. And it was so quiet, had I not been in the silence of the forest, I might have missed it entirely.

I decided I could move much quieter, not to mention faster, without half of Radio Shack chained to my neck, so I ditched my equipment and headed in the direction of the drone. With any luck, I could scope out the operator's position, maybe I.D. him or his base station hideout, then come back with the cavalry later.

What I found was far more dangerous than some geek hiding in a camper. The beast was probably ten feet of teeth and claws when he reared up to his full height, which I hoped to God it didn't. A huge, male grizzly bear. Finding one in The Rockies was all but impossible. Two? Stay away from lightening and start buying lottery tickets. These guys were definitely busing these animals in somehow.

I had moved quietly enough that it hadn't detected me. Any more noise, or worse, had I come in upwind, and Ranger Rob may have had a very unhappy welcoming committee.

The grizzly sat in the underbrush, breathing heavy and hanging its head. It didn't take a degree in wildlife biology to recognize something was wrong. When it rocked itself forward to lope on its way, the problem became horribly clear. The bear's right rear leg was maimed and bloody. The poor creature had to hobble along using its front paws and one rear leg for support. Tracking an animal in this sort of shape would be easy, even if the hunters weren't using a drone.

Bad news was if the bear was here, and the drone was here, that meant the guys with the big guns were here too. Close by anyway. If I didn't think of something quick, I would either be a bear snack or target practice for the poachers. Considering the stakes, I had no doubt they would leave my carcass right here next to the grizzly's if they thought I knew what they were up to.

Time to get a little creative.

The drone seemed to be retracing the same path to and from the bear's location. I guessed it acted as a beacon, bouncing between the poachers and their prey, which meant I should go in the opposite direction. So, of course, I headed straight for them.

I waited until I had a little distance from the bear. I didn't want Mr. Grizzly crawling up my tailpipe. Then I cupped my hands to my mouth and yelled as loud as I could.

"Sarah. If you can hear my voice, call out to me. One of the rescuers will get to you. If you can't call out, come to me."

I waited a few seconds, tromping and beating the bushes, making as much noise as I could, then I repeated the phrase again. I hoped the bear would hear me and hightail it in the other direction. The more distance it had from the poachers, the better.

Within a few minutes, I heard a rustling in the trees. I made a show of talking into my radio, turning up the volume so the beeps and static could be heard.

"I have her. Rescue units assemble at my coordinates." Maybe a little over the top ... and a little too loud. I hoped my award-winning acting didn't get me killed.

"Sarah. We're here to help you. Your parents are safe. We have people all over these wood ..."

I cut off my staged dialogue as four men revealed themselves from the brush. Three of them sported camo so new, neat, and pressed they could have worn it to a board meeting. The fourth one though, he was different. He was dressed in an old, black hunting vest, brown shirt, and fatigue pants. His boots were in the sort of shape that was earned, not purchased. The moment I caught a glimpse of his tattooed head, thick, tangled beard, and dark eyes, I knew who it was. Snake man from the radio shop. The one who owned a black mamba with an affinity for napping in the neighbor's bedroom.

He looked even more dangerous now than he had then. His eyes appraised me, sizing up the threat. Men like him knew only one thing. Violence. I had to make sure he had a clear path out and a reason to use it, or I might wish I'd hung out with the bear.

I keyed the mike on my portable radio and tried to look disappointed. "False alarm. False alarm. Resume search. Repeat, resume search."

I let go of the button on the mike and turned down the volume as if I expected to be interrupted by a barrage of radio traffic and smiled at the oncoming death squad.

"I'm so sorry, guys. We put out a post this evening. All hunting in the area's been suspended. We have a missing girl out here somewhere. We have teams running rescue grids all over the place. I'm surprised you haven't run into one of them before now."

The three Gucci hunters all glanced at each other, looking like they might bolt at any second. Black Beard didn't budge.

"I'll be glad to escort you to your vehicles, if you like. I can even contact you when the ban's been lifted. Do you boys have a number where I can reach you?"

I shifted my gaze to the shuffling trio and pretended not to see them hide their AR-15s behind their backs. These were definitely my huckleberries. If I carried something more than my 9mm and a mini mag-light to take them down, I would have them strung up and screaming for their high-priced lawyers.

"That won't be necessary." Black Beard flashed me a yellow toothed grin, but his eyes remained dead and dark. "We can find our own way out."

I smiled at him, doing my best to reflect a sentiment of cluelessness. "Thank you all so much for understanding. And if you happen to run across one of our teams, please call out and let us know. We don't want any more false alarms."

The band of not so merry killers began to retreat, and I keyed my mike again as they backed away.

"We have four civilians exiting the area." I smiled again and waved to them like the helpful ranger I was. Then, as an afterthought I called out. "The ban should be over soon. We have military choppers inbound. As soon as they get here, we'll find her pretty quick."

If my hunch about them using restricted military frequencies to fly their drones was correct, I hoped it would ground them, at least for a while, but I didn't expect the simple statement to stop all four of them in their tracks.

I stood there for a moment, helpful hand still in the air, wondering if I had just made my last grievous error, then I realized their attention was no longer on me. The three boardroom commandos wore a mask of sheer terror, as they stared off into the forest to my right. I followed their gaze through the trees, squinting through the dimming light. Then I saw it move not more than 20 yards away. All ten feet of the enormous beast that I thought was long gone had circled around for a return engagement. As it heaved itself up to its full height and let out a deafening roar, I knew my mythical search for Sarah was over.

CHAPTER TWENTY-SEVEN

Everything happened at once.

The three Board Room Commandos took off at a run, arms flapping and throats screeching. Black Beard had no such compunction.

He spun with the practiced speed and agility of a true assassin. With one smooth motion, he dropped to a knee, faced the towering wall of claws and teeth, and flipped his AR from his back to a firing position at his shoulder. I barely had time to think much less act. I didn't want to do it, but there was only one logical move for me to make.

With a practiced ease of my own, I drew my 9mm and leveled it at Black Beard's head.

"Fire that weapon, and you die."

Black Beard's eye flicked over to me, but he didn't move a muscle. "That is a grizzly bear. If I don't shoot, we both die."

I didn't relent. Our furry giant dropped down onto all fours and huffed and sniffed at the air, seeming to test his quarry before he made his move.

"Now why would a grizzly bear be in the Colorado Rockies?" I let the question hang in the air for a moment. "If your gun goes off, mine goes off a millisecond later. That's the only threat you need to worry about."

I tilted my head slightly so I could watch the grizzly and Black Beard at the same time. Black Beard, true to his black ops persona, knelt stone still. He didn't fire, but he was not about to lower his weapon either. If our friend charged, all bets were off.

The grizzly hobbled back and forth a few more times, sniffing the air. It inched closer, bobbing its head from side to side on the breeze, almost as if it were homing in on something. Its motions steadied, and the grizzly stopped moving. It had found whatever it was looking ... sniffing for. Bad news was it really pissed him off.

With a chest thrumming roar, our grouchy friend threw all his menace into a terrifying charge. I had less than five seconds to ward off an eight-hundred-pound rolling mass of fur and claws or Black Beard was right. We were both going to die.

"Do not fire!" I shouted each word as I grabbed a canister strapped to my belt. "Do *not* fire that weapon."

I leveled the canister of bear spray toward the charging monster with my left hand while keeping my pistol trained on Black Beard's head with my right. When I pulled the trigger on the cannister, white powder fogged out with a loud hiss, creating a wall of bear spray between us and the charging grizzly.

The sound of its heavy loping steps still crashed through the underbrush, but the fog had obscured my view. I could not tell what the grizzly was doing, how close it was, or even if it still charged in our direction.

I maintained the discharge until all the repellant was gone. A gentle breeze at our backs helped to push the noxious spray toward the bear and away from us. At least that had been in our favor.

After several long moments, the bear's footfalls slowed, and it let out another loud roar. I cringed at the jarring sound, surprised

Black Beard hadn't been startled into firing anyway. For that matter, I was thankful I hadn't either.

When the charging beast didn't emerge from the fog, I knew the spray had done its job. The receding sound of rustling underbrush announced that Elvis had officially left the building. When the fog cleared a second later, Black Beard and I remained in our standoff in an empty forest, and I had no back up. I wasn't sure how much my situation had improved.

He crouched there on his knee, still poised to fire at the absent target. He shifted his eye to me again. I did not relent either. I had a feeling if I dropped my gun, even an inch, Black Beard would roll and fire at the only other big, brown target in the area. He was probably gauging his chances of doing it whether I lowered my weapon or not.

"Bear's gone," he growled. "We done here?"

I huffed. All that bear had to do was hightail it out of the area when it had the chance, but no. He had to show up again and get revenge. Not that I blamed him. Black Beard had done a nasty job on the big guy's leg. I'd want a little payback too.

"I think we both know you don't get to ride off into the sunset."

Black Beard nodded. "Yeah, I think that's pretty clear."

His tone was dangerous. Dripping with meaning I never intended.

"Nice and easy. Raise your right hand away from that trigger, then go ahead and drop your rifle to the ground."

Black Beard complied. He raised his right hand into the air, only holding his weapon with his left. I then realized my mistake. He pivoted hard and swung the butt of the weapon around, using it like an axe handle to strike at my pistol hand. He made contact, batting my hand away. The violence of the blow caused me to fire, but Black Beard had already knocked off my aim.

By the time I managed to recover, Black Beard was up and running. I considered firing at him, even a warning shot, but the blow he had delivered to my hand left it so numb I couldn't pull the trigger. It was a wonder I could hold the gun at all.

I switched the weapon to my left hand and scanned the woods. No sign of Black Beard. He'd vanished like a ghost. It took only a second to realize I now played a game I couldn't win. Hunting Black Beard and potentially three more men with high powered weapons out here in the woods was a losing proposition.

Everything had turned out the way I had planned anyway—more or less. Sure, the bad guys were free, but the grizzly would survive. And I was still alive, which made me the big winner. I had a feeling Black Beard would go to ground, but now I knew who he was. I would hunt him down on my terms, then I'd see how he liked being the prey rather than the predator.

CHAPTER TWENTY-EIGHT

I stared at my phone while I rode the elevator up to my office, hoping to catch up on some work and get my brain engaged in something else besides my screwed-up life. No one would be here. It was Saturday, and not just any Saturday. It was the day of a big event. Everyone would be on site taking care of any last-minute details, everyone but me that is. I had been so self-involved I didn't even realize what day it was until last night. This whole thing with Rob had me tied in so many knots I didn't know which way to turn. And still my phone was blank. No text messages, no voice mails, no nothing. Just a screen as empty as I felt.

The doors opened, and I stepped forward without looking up. Kacey met me with a handful of files that went flying the moment I ran into her.

"I'm so sorry, Denise. I wasn't expecting anyone to be here."

"Ditto." I crouched down to the floor to help her pick up the avalanche of papers. "What are you doing in the office? Shouldn't you be up in Breckenridge taking care of your client?"

Kacey blanched at the use of the word but didn't say anything.

"I had to come back and tidy up some paperwork. I got so

wrapped up in planning the event I forgot to put it all down in a contract."

My eyebrows went up. "We don't have a contract?"

Kacey winced. "Not exactly. I mean Angelo has already paid for everything, and the party is a go. There is just the formality of a signature."

I stood as she shuffled the last of her papers back into the folder and shook my head. "Well, at least you got us paid."

Kacey stood back up as well, not quite meeting my eyes. The guilt train hit me full steam, and I reached out to put a hand on her shoulder.

"Look, I'm sorry I have been so tough on you. Sometimes I can be a little ..."

"Crazy?"

I cocked an eyebrow. "I am trying to apologize, don't push it."

Kacey smiled but tried to cover it by putting a hand over her mouth. "Sorry."

I could not help but grin a little too.

"As I was saying, sometimes I can be a little insecure and overbearing, and yes, maybe a tiny bit crazy. All I am trying to say is you are doing a great job, and you deserve it."

I began to feel a weight on my chest thinking about how everything had spiraled out of my control lately. Kacey let her hand fall to her side, and she was no longer smiling. My eyes began to tear, and it was me who could no longer meet her gaze.

"I have messed everything up so badly. If you hadn't been here to pick up the pieces, I don't know what would have happened. And now Rob is mad at me or maybe in trouble or hurt. I have no idea because he won't call or text me."

A sob heaved out of my chest slamming me firmly in place at rock bottom. Not only had I screwed up every facet of my life, now I was spilling my guts to the cheerleading protégé who *doesn't* want my job.

Kacey dropped her files on the floor and reached out to pull me in for a hug. I resisted at first, but after a second, I laid my head on her shoulder and allowed the tears to flow. I couldn't have stopped them if I wanted to, but maybe getting rid of the overflow would help me cut off the sobbing.

Kacey held me until I regained control and even a few minutes after. Then a minute or two after that it got weird. I backed up and did my best to wipe my eyes without smearing mascara all over my face.

"I am a hot mess. I'm sorry about that."

"Don't be."

Kacey reached out as if to embrace me again, but I held up a hand a chuckled. "No more hugs. I don't want to get started again. I'll be fine."

Kacey gave me a concerned look as she crouched down to retrieve her folder. "You know Jim thinks the world of you. He told me once that this company would have never made it off the ground if you weren't here. You may think you have to walk on water all the time, but trust me, you have nothing to prove. I'm here because you're the best. You don't have to prove it to me or anyone else. We already know it. The only person who seems to doubt it is you."

I let out another chuckle. "And the student becomes the master."

Now it was Kacey's turn to laugh. "Some master I am. I can't even remember to have a client sign a contract."

We both laughed at that.

"You really are doing a terrific job, Kacey. I promise I will be a better mentor in the future."

Kacey smiled and hit the elevator button. "You're already great. Just promise you will be at the party tonight. And forget about Rob. If he is blowing you off, he's not good enough for you. You're Denise Baldwin. No one's allowed to blow you off."

I grinned. "Thanks for the support, but I sort of brought this one on too. He's a keeper— sort of—I think." The sudden admission caught me off guard, and I wasn't sure how to feel about it.

Kacey smiled. "Well, either way, I hope you get everything you deserve."

The elevator doors opened, and Kacey stepped onboard. "Don't forget, tonight. Please be there."

"I will. I promise."

The doors closed, but Kacey's words haunted me. I hope you get everything you deserve. I didn't know if that was a good thing or not. Either way, one thing was for sure. Kacey was right. No one was allowed to blow me off, even if I did deserve it. Especially not a friend. And next time I saw Rob, I would be sure to explain that fact in loud shouting words everyone within earshot would understand.

CHAPTER TWENTY-NINE

After my run in with Black Beard and the grizzly, I spent the entire night working with the Sheriff's department and the FBI to set up a manhunt and sting operation for the poaching ring. We wanted to strike before they had a chance to skip town, which meant pulling an all-nighter to spin them up on what I had uncovered. I was so exhausted when I got home Saturday morning that I shut off my phone and headed straight to bed, uniform and all.

After sleeping through two alarms, I finally dragged myself out of bed, cutting it way too close to the time I was supposed to pick up Denise for the party. I called, sent several texts to let her know I was running late, but no response. While leaving my fifth desperate voicemail, I pulled into her complex, next to her garage, and saw why. Her phone, complete with tire tracks across the smashed screen, lay on the asphalt.

I picked up the phone and shook my head. She would not be in a good mood. First, I was late, then, she destroyed her phone. I hurried back to my Jeep to use the spare garage door opener she had given me in case of emergencies. I hit the button already knowing what I would find.

Sure enough, her car was gone. I pounded my hand on the hood, cursing my own stupidity. How could I do this to her?

I stared into the empty garage contemplating my next steps. Calling her was no longer an option, and unless she had only left a few minutes ago, there was no way I could catch up to her, considering I was almost forty-five minutes late.

I closed the garage door and jumped into my Jeep again. Whether I caught her or not, it didn't matter. I told Denise I'd be there, and that's exactly what I planned to do. I could make up some time on the passes and hopefully get there in time to keep her from being angry enough to pop my head off.

Even if she did, I deserved it. No matter how angry or frustrated I was, she should always be able to depend on me the way I knew I could depend on her. She was always there for me. Always there to listen, help, or just be close when I didn't want to be alone.

I jammed my Jeep into gear and sped out of the parking lot.

I didn't want to believe I had done this on purpose after seeing her with that other guy, but somewhere deep in my mind something had lashed out, even subconsciously. She didn't deserve that. Denise was the best person I knew. She stuck with me through all my drinking and sadness.

And to think, I was considering a relationship with her. Not just considering. I seemed to be obsessed with the thought. Even with the case, Black Beard, and the bear, thoughts of Denise consumed my mind. What if she didn't feel the same way? What if she did? Were we willing to risk our friendship?

Then, as if someone had punched me, I realized it wasn't anger that caused me to be late, it was fear. Fear that this crazy thing might not work out. Fear that I would have to face her and find out.

Once on the highway, I merged into the fast lane, determined to make up time. Scared or not, it was time to face this head on.

Regardless of her current feelings for me, I'd be there for her. I just hoped she wasn't so angry that she didn't want to see me at all.

CHAPTER THIRTY

I paced back to my car again, for the third time, stomping across the dirt parking lot from the landing to the gondola. This time, I had made it almost all the way to the sidewalk before turning around in a mad rush to escape the massive, metal monster. I had no idea what I was going to do. I promised Kacey I would be there for her, and the party had already started. They were all up there on the mountain, relaxing after a day of adventure. And here I was, wearing down my brand-new heels in a frozen, dirt parking lot, because I was too afraid to step into a swinging, swaying, free-floating ball of plexiglass death.

I couldn't even call Kacey to give her a lame excuse; I came down with a case of Ebola or pigeons held me captive for parking violations. Instead, I had left my purse sitting on top of my car when I had pulled out of the garage. Shatterproof glass my ass. And I only ran over the phone with one of my tires.

I slumped against my car and tried to psyche myself up for another run at my nemesis. The freezing metal at my back made my teeth chatter, but I was in the mood to be uncomfortable. Who leaves their best friend hanging like this anyway? I couldn't believe Rob had flaked out on me. Not just flaked out, but hadn't called, sent a text, emailed, nothing. I must have checked my phone a hundred times—before I ran over it, anyway—each time wondering if I should call him. I guess that made two things to put on the no guts, no glory list for today.

Even if I had called, it didn't excuse the fact that he had ditched me—avoided me for almost two days then let me down when I needed him the most. Maybe Rob wasn't the man I thought he was. Or maybe I just didn't deserve a man as good as Rob, and this was the universe delivering the Dear John letter. Either way, I was out here all alone in the frozen wasteland of a winter parking lot, miserable and helpless to even do my job.

I sighed out a big puff of fog and hung my head. Maybe I could find a bar in town that would let me use their phone. I could still use the pigeon excuse.

"Pardon me, ma'am, but does this belong to you?"

My heart skipped a beat at the sound of his voice, and I looked up, unable to believe it could be true.

"Rob? How in the world did you get here?"

"Um, my jeep. How else would I get here?" He grinned.

I didn't want to be happy. I wanted the flutters in my stomach and the catch in my chest to go away. Rob had screwed me over. I wanted to be angry. But there he was, right when I needed him. All decked out in a tux and gorgeous enough to run my hands over every inch of his body. Stupid emotions.

"You know what I meant. Why are you here?"

He walked toward me. "Why? Because I told you I would be here, even if I am a little late."

He held out my mangled cell phone, pinching it between two fingers as if it had been dipped in sewage. "I've been trying to call you for hours. Found this by your garage, so I guess that's why you didn't answer."

A spark of anger flittered its way through all my elation and found a bit of tinder.

"Hours? You haven't called me in days." A mixed cocktail of

anger, hurt, and guilt surged through my veins and hit my brain like a shot of triple tequila. "You can make up another one of your crazy bear stories if you want to, but it's obvious you've been avoiding me."

His eyebrows went up. "You may not believe this but—"

I held up my hand. "Whatever. That night you saw me downtown, it's wasn't what it looked like. I mean, it was, but it wasn't." My voice got louder as my emotions took hold. "If you were mad, fine, but you should have called or came over so we could talk instead of ignoring me. That's not what—"

Rob put a finger on my lips and shook his head. "Let's not argue. You have a job to do, and I came here to support my best friend. Let's just agree to put this all aside for now and have a nice evening. We can talk about—stuff later."

I set my jaw and prepared to talk about it now whether he liked it or not, but when I looked into his eyes, I caught myself. There was no anger there. No betrayal or frustration. There was only sadness and that made me feel the worst of all.

"But I want to talk about—"

"Either we put it to the side, or I'm leaving. That's the deal."

I thought about it for a minute, half furious that I couldn't spew out explanations and maybe a little blame, but he had me against a wall. If I wanted to get up to that party, I needed Rob's help.

"Fine," I huffed. "You win. No talking about ..."

Rob eyed me, catching my thinly veiled attempt to make a statement anyway.

I sighed again.

"No talking about stuff, whatever." I folded my arms against the frigid air and pouted. "You still didn't call."

"If it makes any difference, I had a good reason."

I resisted the urge to ask the obvious question. Unfortunately, the big jerk knew me well enough to know I would not be able to resist it for long, so he just stood there staring at me, drawing out the agonizing silence.

"All right, fine," I finally said. "What was your reason?"

Rob grinned. I knew he was doing it on purpose.

"I had a break in the case. Almost busted one of the poachers out in the woods."

My jaw dropped open, and I reached out to punch him in the arm. "That's not better. I can't believe you didn't call to tell me. What happened?"

Rob took a breath to speak, then paused, looking off to the side as if reconsidering what he was going to say.

"Actually, there's a lot to tell. There really was a bear."

"What?" My eyes went wide.

"It was a grizzly bear. It attacked. There was lots of bear spray and guns and … never mind. I'll tell you about it later. We need to get going. Short story is I had to let the bad guy go. I've been working all day with the FBI and the Sheriff's Department to hunt the guy down. That's why I've been too busy to call."

I groaned inwardly, regretting every suspicious thought I had. "So, did they find him?"

Rob smiled. "I don't know yet. I left. Some things are more important than multi-jurisdictional manhunts."

I wanted to cry. Never in my life did I think the word multi-jurisdictional would be used in one of the nicest things anyone had ever said to me.

I leapt forward and threw my arms around him, pressing my head to his chest. "You're the greatest guy in the world."

Rob wrapped his arms around me as well, and all of a sudden, I was keenly aware of every rippled muscle in his body. I pulled him in tighter, inhaling his after shave and soaking in his radiating heat. I didn't want to let go, but if we stayed like this much longer, we might have a whole new excuse for not making it to the party.

Rob must have felt the same way because he stepped back

and looked down into my eyes. His face was so warm and kind I wanted to melt into his dimples.

"So, how about you, me, and that beautiful dress head on up to this little soiree?"

I smiled. "Oh, this old thing?" I unzipped my coat so he could see the whole ensemble.

His eyes scanned me up and down.

"Wow…" He smiled. "You look amazing. I am going to make a lot of guys jealous at this party"

The word party felt like a smack in the face and reminded me of the chrome monster on the other side of the parking lot, waiting to eat me. My heart sped up and tried to make a quick exit out of my chest. "I don't think I can go. I've been down here for almost an hour trying to get up the courage to get on that stupid gondola. The operator probably thinks I'm Rainman."

Rob laughed and took my hand. "I promised to get you to that party, and that's what I'm going to do. Just relax and leave it to me."

CHAPTER THIRTY-ONE

"How did you know there was a road all the way to the top of the mountain?" I took Rob's hand and climbed out of his Jeep while he held the door, being careful not to slip on the icy ground.

"I figured their supplies and staff got up here somehow. I couldn't imagine them all packing into the gondola with a delivery truck and a cleaning cart."

The visual brought a chuckle to my lips. "Why didn't I think of that?"

"Probably because the thought of getting on that stupid contraption had you so frazzled you couldn't see straight." Rob winked. "The real trick was getting them to leave the gates open for me. They don't want just anyone wandering up their secret path. Sort of ruins the illusion. I told them I was accessing their emergency egress routes, and if any of them were blocked, I would have to cite them with a violation."

I stopped in my tracks. "No, you did not. Rob, this party is incredibly important to Kacey. How could you do something like that?"

"Relax." He smirked. "They didn't know me, and it was just a phone call. If they want to know why we're up here, I'll tell them we happened upon an open driveway and decided to see where it led."

I narrowed my eyes at him but couldn't help but grin. He had gone to a lot of trouble to accommodate my crazy, phobic necessities. And I thought he had let me down altogether. With every gallant act, he twisted the guilt dagger a little tighter. I owed him big. Paying him back was going to require more than picking up a dinner tab. I would have to think of something creative. The less than pure thoughts that invaded my mind were so shocking Netflix would have banned them.

I did my best to hide my flushing face and pulled him closer, enjoying the warmth and his flexing muscle as I wrapped my hand around his arm. "You're too much. You know that?" We made our way to what looked like a cinderblock wall made of ice. It was actually a façade that masked a huge, insulated dome housing the extraordinary structure we were here to visit. Two doormen waited for us, wearing big white parkas with furry hoods. The coats looked like pure heaven considering the sub-arctic temperatures Rob and I endured to cross the walkway. They were so thick, they made ours look like papier-mâché.

When we approached, they directed us to a window off to their left where we traded our pretend jackets for a twin set to the doormen's.

Rob donned his and then took mine. I thought he was going to hold it for me, but he threw it over his arm instead.

"What are you doing? It's cold." I rubbed my arms.

He eyed me top to bottom and grinned. "It's just a shame we have to cover all of that up. You really do look amazing tonight. If we weren't friends..."

He finished the statement with a wink.

I spun in a little circle, letting him take a long look at the slinky, black dress I had picked for the evening. It had an open back, a tempting front, and hugged my every curve. "If we weren't such good friends, I might just let you."

As soon as I stopped, I jabbed him in the shoulder. "Now give me my coat. I'm freezing."

Rob chuckled and held out the long, white Eskimo parka. It was surprisingly comfortable. Faux fur lined and a bit bulky, but it was like wearing a down comforter straight out of the dryer.

I wondered if it might be too warm once we were inside, but as soon as the doormen opened the entrance of the frozen night-club, I wondered if our new indoor outer wear would be enough.

Rob took my hand, and we stepped inside, emerging through a blast of icy cold fog that further served as a barrier to the outside air. The interior took my breath away—literally.

The frigid air filled my nose and throat, and I squinted as my eyes adjusted to the frosty air. Rob flipped his hood up and helped me with mine. It felt like a furry, open-faced astronaut's helmet, but it definitely helped to cut the chill.

The place was huge. Much larger than I could have imagined and constructed entirely of ice. Every wall, every countertop looked as if it had been carved out of glass. Colored lights gleamed beneath the surface, giving the entire place an ethereal glow. The only thing made of actual glass was a champagne pyramid so high, I had to wonder how they built it. The beveraged structure must have contained thousands of glasses and who knew how many gallons of champagne. When I had told Kacey to go over-the-top, she took my advice and injected it with steroids. This party was so over-the-top it gave a whole new meaning to over-the-top. The only problem now would be finding a way to outdo it next year.

"Hey." Kacey's chronically cheerful voice emerged from the din of conversations all around us. We both turned to see her approach from the ice top bar several yards away, wearing the same Nordic parka issued to everyone at the party. "I'm so glad you made it. I was starting to worry you wouldn't come."

I smiled and pulled her in for a hug. "I wouldn't miss this for the world. This is amazing, Kacey. I couldn't have done better myself."

"Thanks." She beamed. "That means a lot coming from you."

"I mean it." I swept my arm around the room. "This is incredible. And you managed to pull this all together in a week. Unheard of."

Kacey looked down at the floor, and I swear I saw her blush. Could this girl get any more sickeningly humble? "I had a lot of help. My uncle had everything ready to go, so my part was easy."

"Still, you found a great solution to an impossible problem. Take some credit for it. You did a fantastic job."

"Thanks." She smiled.

"Hey, you remember Rob, from the other night downtown?" The mere mention of that evening was enough to make my stomach turn.

She looked up at his face as if recognizing him for the first time. "Oh, yes." She reached out to shake Rob's hand, and I could see that I had just dropped a big, old, awkward grenade in the middle of our threesome.

"Look, I feel like I need to apologize to the both of you about that night. I am ashamed at how I handled myself and a potential client. If I ever see Brett again, I will owe him an apology as well, at least for part of the evening."

I thought back to the way I had led him on and the way he had reacted when I decided to leave. He had earned every bit of my wine drenched parting on his own, but I should have handled the whole encounter better. For that, I was sorry.

Kacey perked up at the sound of Brett's name. Not the reaction I expected in the midst of my groveling. But pretty much everything perked Kacey up, so why not this too?

Her eyes searched the room and then she pointed to a huddled group of parkas across the way. "Brett's here. You can talk to him if you want to. I guess Angelo uses his drones to track his vacation expeditions. Supposed to be some sort of secret weapon. I don't know why. It just takes picture of people's vacations, right? Big deal. I guess they're beta testing some new units here in the mountains to see how they do in higher elevations. That's why Brett was here."

I glanced at Brett and his group of friends. Should I apologize? Yes. Did I want to do it right this second? Well …

Thankfully Rob came to my rescue once again. "Hold on a second. Your client does what?"

"Angelo organizes exclusive tours and vacations to unusual destinations for people who have a lot of money," I said. "Like the kind of money you and I could only dream about."

"And this Angelo happens to be in cahoots with someone who specializes in drones?"

I nodded, feeling my eyebrows knit together as I tried to work out where he was going with this.

"Kacey, would you excuse us for a minute?" He pulled me away without waiting for her to answer and hurried us off to a spot where no one would hear us.

"What's wrong with you?" I looked around, trying to figure out what had Rob so worked up.

"This party is what's wrong." He lowered his voice to a hushed hiss. "This place is full of fat-cat adventurers looking for a thrill, and I think your client is the kingfish who gives it to them. I think he's the guy I've been looking for all along."

CHAPTER THIRTY-TWO

"What do you mean?" I took a step back and shook my head. "Angelo can't be the guy you're looking for."

"It's him. It all makes sense," Rob said.

"But you've been investigating a poaching ring," I said, "not a tourism specialist."

"Then again, what would my tourism business be without a hook, something new to draw people in?" I went to turn toward the familiar voice, but Angelo's hand clamped down on my shoulder like a vice, holding me in place. Apparently, we hadn't moved far enough to escape *all* the prying ears at the party.

Rob stepped toward him, but Angelo countered, shoving my body in the way.

"Careful now." He slid something beneath my parka and jabbed something against my side. "That is a 9mm Luger. It's nothing fancy, but I promise I can pull the trigger fast enough to put a half a dozen holes through that pretty dress of yours before your boyfriend can take a breath."

"You don't want to do this, Angelo." I tried to keep my voice from cracking. "Put the gun away, and we can talk."

He pressed the gun harder into my side. "Talk? I think were past the point of talking."

Rob's face was a mask of terror and fury. He showed his hands without raising them as if to tell Angelo he wouldn't try anything either.

"Good." The pressure of the gun against my side relaxed a little, but Angelo's hand remained clamped over my shoulder. "Now we are all going to move to the door behind the bar. You will not make a scene or call any undue attention to us. We are going to exit quietly and be on our merry way."

Angelo gave me a little shove to get us moving in the right direction. "You first, hero." He looked at Rob. "I want you where I can see you."

Rob nodded, keeping his hands out while he made his way through the maze of icy tables and parka-clad party goers.

"I must admit, I was surprised when my associate told me about a confrontation he had had with a ranger in the forest last night." He spoke in my ear just loud enough so only I could hear him. "Imagine my surprise when my associate noticed the very same ranger here at our little party this evening. I would like to know how your boyfriend made the connection so quickly, but I feel the best course of action right now is for all of us to make a hasty retreat."

The jovial chatter and booming music made the moment feel all the more surreal. Here we were, being held at gunpoint in the middle of a party, and no one knew. They went on drinking, laughing, and dancing, having no idea I was inches away from a horrible death. The thought seemed to short circuit something in my head, and I couldn't catch my breath. My heart pounded, and I began to wheeze in and out at the rate of a hummingbird's wings.

"Take it easy now, Denise." Angelo must have felt the tension rising in my body. "We're almost there. No one has to get hurt as long as you both cooperate and—"

Brett Hamilton barged through, invading every inch of my personal space to stand so close I could smell the booze reeking off his breath.

"Well, well. Moving up in the world, are we?" He slurred all his syllables together until they formed a sort of single word. "Fair warning, Angelo. As soon as you think you've got this sweet little piece in the bag, she'll run, leaving you with your dick in your hand."

I turned my head away, trying to avoid getting close to his face. I saw Rob standing behind him, ready to peel Brett away like the rind on an orange, but I shook my head in quick jerks, hoping to keep him from causing a scene—and inviting Angelo to use his Luger.

"I'm sorry about the other night, Brett. Let me take care of Angelo here and then you and I can have a drink."

I cringed at how bad that sounded. Brett did not miss the connotations either.

"How 'bout you take care of me first." He slipped forward, eating up the inch or so of space that remained between us and pressed his body against mine. "How 'bout I put my dick in your hand instead."

I raised my face to his and shot him a rueful smile. When he smiled, I shoved him back and connected my right hook to his jaw. Gun or no gun, no one got away with talking to me like that.

So much for not making a scene. Brett staggered, cartwheeling his arms like a drunken acrobat. His feet could not keep up with his butt as he tumbled back, and his body crashed into the pyramid of champagne glasses like a bowling ball hitting ... well, champagne glasses. They came down like a slow-motion building demolition, imploding upon the catalyst. The deafening sound resembled that of a thousand chandeliers being dropped from the sky. All conversation stopped. Even the music came to a halt, then raucous laughter filled the air. Even Angelo laughed behind me, but he tightened his grip on my shoulder. The only people not laughing were Brett and Rob. They both wore murderous expressions. I was glad only one of them was meant for me.

"Let's get going." Angelo gave me a shove. "I don't think either of us wants to be here when young Brett frees himself from that mess."

I complied, and Rob turned to continue leading us out. The laughter still rang in my ears as we disappeared through the rear exit to emerge into the fading light of the evening.

The temperature outside almost matched the frigid environment inside the ice bar. For once, I was glad to be wearing the world's heaviest coat.

Much to my surprise, Angelo was shedding his behind me, exposing himself to the glacial air. A quick glance around told me why. Sitting just to our left was a charcoal gray McLaren 720s. A supercar that made Porsche cower in a puddle of its own transmission fluid and had no business being up in the mountains in the middle of winter. The cab was also about as roomy as a pair of extra small Spanx. No elbowroom for an Eskimo parka.

"Take off that ridiculous thing and get in the car." He yanked my coat down by the collar and tore it off toward the ground before latching his hand onto my shoulder again.

Rob took a step toward us, and I felt the gun press harder into my side.

"Rob, no! Stay back," I shouted.

Angelo eyed him and shook his head. "Now, now hero. You have done so good. Don't ruin things."

He pulled me toward the driver's side of the car and opened the door.

"Take care of him, then bring the gondola down and make sure the control house is wrecked for good. I don't want anyone getting cute and following us out."

At first, I thought he was talking to Rob, which made no sense, then a figure emerged out of the shadows next to the wall.

A huge man wearing insulated camo and a lot of tattoos. He had a long, shaggy, black beard and dark, dead eyes. He must have been standing there the whole time, and I hadn't noticed him. I could see now that Rob had, and something about the mix of dread and anger in his eyes spoke of a sort of unwelcome familiarity. All at once, I felt more worried for Rob's life than my own.

I choked down the tears trying to escape. "Let us go! You can leave. I won't say anything. Just go."

"Sorry, can't do that." Angelo shoved me down and into the door of the car, forcing me over the console to the passenger-side seat.

"Rob!" I couldn't stop the tears now. "Let him go, Angelo!"

"Don't take too long." Angelo said to the creepy guy, unfazed by my screaming. "We have a plane to catch if we're going to make it out of the country by this evening."

CHAPTER THIRTY-THREE

Black Beard prowled out around me. "Hey there, Boy Scout."

I watched Angelo pull away with Denise. Her terrified eyes were trained on me as he crept by, over-revving his engine and spinning his wheels on the icy roadway. I didn't miss the smirk on Angelo's smug face either. I had to find a way to catch them. He would not leave this mountain, much less the country, with Denise in tow.

"You and I have some unfinished business." Black Beard's rough voice jerked my attention away from the car, which fishtailed within inches of the guardrail. As if holding her at gunpoint wasn't enough reason to worry.

"I don't have time to play with you right now." I glared at the rough-cut man, looking for the best way to get past him. "If your boss wanted to stop me, he should have used his gun."

Black Beard let out a chuckle. "You misunderstand. Angelo Scalari is not my boss. He is my business associate, and he left you at my request."

Before I could make a move, he reached behind his back and drew out a Bowie knife large enough to make Crocodile Dundee jealous.

"Like I said, you and I have unfinished business to attend to. I don't mind using a gun now and then, but when it's personal, I like to get my hands dirty."

Black Beard lowered himself into a half crouch and began to circle me, brandishing his knife in the air.

I countered his move by circling in the opposite direction, realizing too late that he wanted to steer my back to the wall of the building. Once I had no escape, he would pounce, using his size and weight to pin me in. That idea did not sound appealing. I sidestepped in the other direction, catching him off guard enough to escape his trap.

What I really needed was a weapon. Something to fight with or at least defend myself against his blade.

My gaze flicked along the ground. Nothing but white powder and a little gravel. Unless we switched to a snowball fight, I was out of luck. My only chance was to run for it, although I didn't see a way I could escape his blade completely. I would have to try a wild dive and hope he didn't slice too deep. Maybe my Nanook jacket was stab proof too.

Just as I prepared to make my move, the back door of the club burst open, and a man tumbled out. He seemed to be in a fistfight with the business end of a mop. The man flailed on the ground, trying to wrestle the unruly octopus off of his face. It took a moment to realize the handle was still in the hands of some unseen janitorial assailant. Even Black Beard paused to take in the spectacle. As soon as the man got to his feet, he jerked a mop out of his assailant's hand and slammed the door, sealing my escape shut for the second time.

"Where is she? Where's that bitch?"

It took me a moment to recognize him, but his champagne drenched tux was a dead giveaway. It was Denise's not-so-friend, Brett from inside.

He pointed the mop handle at my face and demanded an

answer. "Where did she go? Tell me, or so help me, I will kick your ass right here."

I nodded to the burly, armed pirate standing behind him. "You're going to have to get in line, bud."

When he turned toward Black Beard, I snatched the mop out of his hand and braced it on the ground. One quick stomp, and the head snapped off, leaving me a makeshift staff. I was used to working with a baton, but beggars can't be choosers. The sudden action mixed with the sight of Black Beard's blade was enough to make the champagne fan squeak like a mouse. He jumped back so far, I half expected him to leap into my arms.

"Beat it, drone boy." Black Beard grabbed his shoulder and threw him to the side. "This has nothing to do with you."

Brett tripped, rolled through the snow, recovered, and never stopped running.

Black Beard was finished toying around too. He lunged in low and fast, trying to gut me with the first strike. I parried it with my mop handle and managed a quick down-strike to the top of his head.

The blow was hard enough to make him stagger and hold his knife out in front of him, waving it as if the world had just shifted off axis without telling him.

A thick line of blood rose on his scalp and then ran down his face. My blow hadn't just dazed him, it had split the smooth skin like an onion.

Black Beard reached up to feel the gash and then looked at me in disbelief. I shrugged and gave my staff a little spin. Not my most intelligent move—especially when wearing a coat bulky enough to add another zip code.

My staff spun half-way round, got caught in the bottom of the jacket, and almost fell out of my hand. In my struggle to recover, Black Beard darted in again, moving much faster than I gave him credit for. He swiped his knife wide, and I didn't have a chance to block it. The blade sank into the flesh on my arm, leaving a deep cut across my left bicep.

"Now we're even." He chuckled. "Time to finish so I can head down to meet your girlfriend."

I took a step back and shed the parka. If I planned to win this fight, I couldn't get tangled up in every swing. Black Beard feigned left toward my injured arm before I got the coat all the way off. I knew he would. This time I was ready for him. In one deft move, I flipped the coat into his face then swept my mop handle around to meet him when he charged to the right instead. The thick, wooden handle caught him at the jaw. He staggered forward, knife hand down, so I delivered a fast strike to his knuckles, dislodging his blade before I spun the makeshift staff up and into his face. Staggering was no longer an option. Black Beard went down in a heap.

I stood ready to deliver another hard blow if he were playing possum, but the state of his jaw—and his teeth—told me faking was not all that necessary.

I reached down and grabbed his giant knife, then patted him down in search of other weapons. I found a smaller one in his boot. They always have one in the boot. Black Beard would be out for a while but not forever. I didn't want to leave him to go marauding back through the party. On the other hand, I didn't have time to mess with him either. Every second I stood there was another second Denise got farther away. I decided to leave him and run. I had his weapons, and if I was going to catch Denise, I would have to do something drastic. At this rate, drastic was getting to be my middle name.

CHAPTER THIRTY-FOUR

"You're a monster." I reached over and managed to jam the seatbelt into the little, red clip at my hip. "What is wrong with you? What's that guy going to do with Rob?" I screamed.

I choked back the tears as anger rose. "I hope you know he's an I.S.B. agent. That's like the F.B.I. of the Park Rangers, in case you didn't know. He is probably arresting your freaky mountain man right now."

Angelo let out a chuckle but cut it off short when his supercar slid out of control and threatened to go careening off the road for the hundredth time. He managed to wrestle the grossly overpowered car straight again and do his best to crawl down the icy switchbacks.

"I'm afraid Ruddy is a bit of a handful. There is a reason he leads my expeditions. Even an armed snob outfitted with high-powered lawyers would think twice about crossing him."

"I can't believe you kill endangered animals. What kind of sick bastard does something like that?" I thought about hitting him. Punching, scratching, gouging—anything to vent my disgust, betrayal, and anger—but the gun he held in his hand stopped me from trying it. That and the fact that he was barely keeping his stupid car under control. "As soon as I get out of this thing, I'm calling the cops. How did you think you were going to get away with this?"

Angelo shot me a sideways glance and waved his pistol at me as if that were supposed to be some kind of answer.

"What? You're going to shoot me?" I let out an exasperated breath. "I know you. You're not dumb enough to shoot someone. People like you leave that kind of stuff to goons like ... what was your freak's name?"

"His name is Ruddy, and you may want to ask yourself why I'm so willing to tell you if I'm planning to let you go. If you don't shut up, I may shoot you just for a little peace and quiet down the mountain."

I scoffed. "You don't have the balls. You wouldn't soil your precious car. If you did, what would you use to impress all the girls with? If you had the equipment to impress them on your own, you wouldn't drive a chick magnet like this up in the snow."

A little voice inside me screamed for me to shut my mouth, but my hostility seemed to take on a life of its own. Being taken hostage and held at gunpoint. Rob being left in the hands of a lunatic. Everything careened out of control like this stupid car. The only thing I could do was hurl insults. And even those were pretty weak. Chick magnet? Where had that come from?

Angelo cranked the wheel with his right hand while holding the pistol with his left, pointing it at me across his body as he fought to straighten the car. He gave it a little too much gas, which in this case was pretty much any gas at all, and the rear of the car swung around like a punch-drunk boxer. I clenched everything clenchable and held onto the dash as Angelo overcorrected and ran the car into a shallow drift. The McLaren ground to a halt with an icy crunch, and I saw my chance to escape.

I wished I'd spent less time crafting witty insults and more time looking for the door handle. It took me a moment to find it, but when I did, I threw the door open and dove out—or at least I tried to. Safety conscious as always, I had fastened my seatbelt, and when I made my stuntwoman move, it hung me up like a clothesline. The door bounced back, and I was left no choice but to turn and fumble with the safety snare that had trapped me in place.

That's when Angelo fired the Luger.

I screamed at the deafening sound and raised my hands to the sides my head, as if that would somehow block the bullets from entering my skull. My ears rang, and the car's engine fell to an idle. I lowered my arms at a slow, almost glacial speed, daring to glance in Angelo's direction out of the corner of my eye.

He sat calm and motionless, still pointing the gun in my direction while appraising me with cold, heartless eyes. Eyes that told me everything I knew about him was a sham. This man was a killer through and through. I would never make it to a phone to call the police. I wasn't even going to make it out of this car.

"If you would be so kind as to close the door …" He paused motioning toward the handle. "I am in a bit of a hurry."

A little sob escaped my lips as I reached out to pull the door closed. I didn't want to cry again. Not in front of him. He didn't deserve the satisfaction of knowing he had frightened me to the point of tears, but I couldn't help it. As soon as the door was closed, I turned my head toward the side window. At least I didn't have to let him see me.

"There is something you should know about this car." He chuckled out a dry laugh and put the car in gear. With a lurch, we started moving again. "It's a rental."

I held in another sob and stared up the mountainside. Nothing short of a miracle would save me now. Then Rob's Jeep burst out of the trees in front of us, and we broadsided him before Angelo could even touch the brakes.

CHAPTER THIRTY-FIVE

I struggled to make sense of what was happening. Everything blurred together. I tried to blink away the haze, and inch by inch, the world around me emerged. A Jeep laying on its side in the ditch. A rumbling engine and an angry sounding hiss. The hood in front of me was bent up and fractured, and my chest hurt where my seatbelt crossed my sternum.

"Denise, can you hear me? Are you okay?"

I felt a gentle, warm hand on my cheek and turned my head toward the voice. Rob crouched next to me. Where had he come from? Then the memory came to me in a flash. Rob careening straight down the mountain, Angelo having no time to stop, us ramming Rob's jeep and flipping him over. Fear and worry hit me all at once, slapping me into reality.

"Rob, are you hurt? What did you do? How did you get down here?"

I looked up to see his forehead bleeding and a huge gash on his arm. "You *are* hurt."

He shook his head and reached over me to pop my seatbelt free. "I'm fine. Only part of this is from the crash. We need to get you out of this car though."

Thoughts of Angelo and his gun made me jerk around in a panic. He would kill us both. I opened my mouth to warn Rob, but there was no need. Angelo was slumped over the steering wheel, his head bloodied much worse than Rob's.

"Angelo should always take the time to wear his seatbelt." Rob smiled. "Like someone else I know."

I winced at the spider-webbed glass above Angelo's head.

Rob's strong hands helped me up and steadied me as I found my footing. I glanced around our surroundings, looking for any other people or backup. Rob had come alone.

"He has a gun. If he wakes up ..."

Rob pulled me in close to him and held my head to his chest. "I have his gun. It's all over. We just need to get some help."

He loosened his grip on me and looked down into my eyes. "I was so afraid he would hurt you, and I would lose you forever. And that thought... well..." He put his hand on my cheek and paused. "I don't want to think about it anymore. Are you all right?" He looked me over.

Him asking me if I was all right with blood all over his face made me want to laugh and cry at the same time. He was the one who had just about killed himself.

"I'm fine, but you're crazy. You could have died pulling a stunt like that."

Rob shrugged. "Just so happens I've had a little practice skiing down mountainsides in my Jeep lately. I'm sort of getting used to it."

"Next time we go out, I am driving." I wrapped my arms around him and pulled him tight. "Thank you for coming to get me. I don't know what he would have done if ..." I couldn't finish the statement.

Rob held me close. It felt so good. In this moment, everything felt right in the world. Even out here, shivering in the bitter cold amidst the aftermath of what could have been the end of both of our lives.

"Will you be all right here for just a second?" Rob loosened his embrace to look down at me. "I need to see if I can find Angelo's cell phone. I must have lost mine during the ..." He paused. "During my discussion with the man at the resort."

I screwed up my face. "A discussion?"

"Yeah." Rob shrugged. "We talked, then did some other stuff. It's not important. You're safe, and the bad guys lost."

I gave him a slow nod. "You will have to tell me about the other stuff later. For now, go get that bastard's cell phone. I don't want any of those people getting away on the gondola."

Rob let me go and took a step back, allowing his hands to slip down my arms and linger at my fingers as if he wasn't quite ready to part.

"No chance of that. I ran into Kacey on my way out. I told her to call the cops and fill them in. They'll be waiting at the bottom for anyone who thinks they can make a clean getaway."

I smiled. "And did you tell her about your pursuit plan?"

He winced. "I was in a hurry. I may have forgotten to tell her about Angelo and your little side trip down the mountain. That's why I need the cell phone."

I shook my head and let go of his hand. "Be careful."

Rob smiled and nodded at me while stepping round to the driver's side of the car. Before he got there, the engine roared to life with a hiss and a squeal, making me jump back. The McLaren peeled out in a rush of ice and snow with Angelo behind the wheel.

Rob and I watched in shock as the car swished and swayed its way down the switchback road. I kept willing Angelo to lose control. Not that I wanted him to die. Maybe just get stuck and make a run for it—and meet a hungry bear or something.

All my mental efforts were to no avail. Despite his injuries and the condition of the vehicle, Angelo managed to keep his stupid car on the road all the way down until he was out of sight.

"Well, that just happened." I wrapped my arms around

myself, already feeling the bitter cold biting through the thin material of my dress. "Now what are we going to do?"

Rob looked at me. I felt pretty calm considering the circumstances, but when I saw Rob's expression, my worry meter pegged out at an eleven. "The sun is down. The wind is picking up, and no one knows we're out here."

CHAPTER THIRTY-SIX

Rob kicked the door to a small, warming cabin. It flew open with a bang, and he carried me across the threshold. He was in no way outfitted for freezing temperatures with nothing but his suit and a pair of stylish loafers to protect him against the elements. Compared to me though, he was set for an overnight in the arctic.

While my thin dress made me look hot in one way, it did nothing to stop the frigid temperatures from cutting through to my skin, even with the blanket he found for me. My high heels made nice ice picks, but the smooth soles made them useless on the slippery ground. Rob had been forced to carry me after the first few minutes. By the time we made it to the warming cabin, I was curled up against him like a kitten trying to leach all the heat out of his chest and arms that I could.

"I have to put you down for just a minute."

"You're not going to carry me around all night?" I said through shivering teeth.

"I can if you want me to, but I bet you'd rather I got the fire going." He set me on a couch that faced a wood burning stove and covered me with a few other blankets that laid about the hut.

"Yes, please." I wrapped the blankets around me as tightly as I could with my numb hands.

"It looks like the embers are still hot from earlier. People from the resort must have stoked the stoves for day hikers. I'm sure they figured no one in their right mind would be out in this weather at night."

They would be right except for the psycho-poacher and his low-speed supercar escape attempt.

"It's a good thing you saw those cross-country ski tracks when you did, or we would have never found this place." I winced at the thought of being stranded outside.

"You can thank my job and years of tracking down miscreants." Rob opened the stove door, and I could see the dim, orange remnants of an earlier fire. The meager warmth that escaped from the opening made me want to crawl inside, Hansel and Gretel style, and curl up for a nap.

With a few jabs of a poker, Rob transformed the coals into an angry, red glow. He threw on a few logs from a woodpile nearby and within seconds the fire was roaring. It felt so good, I almost opened up my blankets to soak in the heat. But my body shivered, and I changed my mind.

"This place will be toasty as a toaster in a few minutes."

I scrunched my face up at him. "Toasty as a toaster? That has to be the worst metaphor I have ever heard."

He raised his eyebrows. "I believe you mean the worst simile you have ever heard."

"It's never too cold for me to punch you."

Rob laughed, standing near the fireplace, rubbing his arms. He had given me all the blankets and taken none for himself, and the fire wasn't warming up fast enough to knock the chill out of the air.

"Come down here." I pulled my knees up close to my chest and then opened up an arm to let him into my blanket sanctum.

"Aren't you supposed to be some sort of outdoor expert? Don't you know body heat is the best way to get warm?"

Rob laughed and snuggled in next to me, wrapping his arms around me and pulling me in close to his chest.

"Actually, the best way to share body heat is skin to skin."

I blinked at him.

"I'm just reciting the facts. Clothes only serve as a barrier to the transfer of body heat. Studies have shown that by removing most of your clothing in a hypothermic emergency, you increase your chances of survival by ninety-two percent."

"Most of your clothes?" I snorted. "You're so hot when you recite survival statistics."

"Personally, I would go with all the clothes, just to be on the safe side."

"Over-achiever." I laughed and looked up at him.

Rob laughed too, but then he caught my eye. Our laughter dwindled and something in his gaze turned to desire. I felt it too. My heart pounded in my chest while I gripped his jacket, pulling him closer as I tried to keep my breathing under control. My emotions had turned into a runaway wildfire igniting every nerve in my body.

Rob's face lingered close to mine, his breath on my lips. My gaze fluttered down to his mouth, inviting him, beckoning him in. Still he waited, the heat between us building, the intensity in his eyes growing.

Just when I thought I could stand it no more, when I thought I would break and surge forward on my own, he kissed me. Gentle at first, then came something more. Something so full of desire and emotion everything else faded away. I became lost in his kiss and the longing that fueled it. His strong grip held me tight, raising the heat in my emotions higher than I thought possible. Nothing else mattered. The cold, the car chase, the party, the psychotic killers—none of it felt important anymore.

Being here with Rob, someone who had always been there for me and who knew me better than anyone else. That's what counted.

Rob pulled away just enough to part our lips and rested his forehead against mine.

"There is something I have to tell you." He let out a breath.

Sudden worry threatened to infect the moment. Maybe he didn't feel the same as I did. Could this connection be a figment of my imagination? He probably wanted to stay friends. My heart now raced with panic, and I tried to lean away, but Rob held me fast, not letting me escape. I looked at him. Questioning his eyes.

"What is it?" The words came out so soft they were barely audible. Whatever he had to say, I could handle it. Part of me, well, all me, wanted to cover my ears and disappear back into his arms.

"What I said earlier," he began, and I braced myself for the worst, "about being ninety-two percent more likely to survive hypothermia if you took off your clothes? I made that up. I have no idea how much it improves your chances; I just wanted to get you naked."

I blinked at him, then smacked him in the chest.

He choked before blustering out a laugh. "I just didn't want us to have any lies between us."

I tried to keep my expression from cracking, but it didn't work. I let out a laugh of my own and swung myself over to straddle his lap. "Who am I to argue with a professional?" I slipped my dress over my head and smiled at him. He raised his eyebrows and grinned before pulling me in close to share enough heat to last us a lifetime.

CHAPTER THIRTY-SEVEN

I finished talking and sat back in the chair in Jim's office. Kacey covered her mouth with her hands and took in a quick gasp of air. It was Monday, and the first time I had seen everyone since the crazy events at the party. We were comparing notes. Kacey told me about the police showing up to storm the castle. Even though the guest list consisted of lowlife poachers, they didn't have the evidence to detain them. Not yet anyway. They did, however, record every name as a person of interest, putting them firmly on the ISB radar.

Brett and Ruddy were another matter. They both had tried to make a run for it on foot, but Brett collapsed about a hundred yards from the lodge. Ruddy made it farther. Despite the injuries he suffered during his *discussion* with Rob, it took the better part of a day and a half to flush him out of the frozen mountainside. In the end, the harsh climate got the best of him too.

"I can't believe he shot at you." Kacey's eyes were wide enough to drive her Volkswagen through. "How did you get away from him?"

Jim leaned against his desk, facing the two of us, looking every bit as shocked and worried as Kacey.

I adjusted myself in Jim's guest chair and shrugged. "Turns out my knight in shining armor drives a Jeep. Rob tobogganed it straight down the mountain and took Angelo out. Good thing I had my seatbelt on, or my head would have smashed the windshield like his."

Kacey's hands went from her face to her heart. "Wow. That's incredible. I'm so glad you're all right."

"Knock, knock." I turned to see Rob poking his head into the office. He had his arm in a sling and a bandage on his head, but as far as I was concerned, he had never looked more handsome.

"What are you guys talking about?"

Kacey let out a screech, then scurried over to envelop Rob in an emphatic hug. Rob arched an eyebrow, then looped his free arm around her in return. "Have you been telling wild stories about me again?"

I shrugged. "Could have been wilder. I left out the part about you fighting grizzlies, disarming the gondola monster, and your mop handle ninja tactics." I grinned and shot him a wink as images of our time in the cabin sent shivers through every inch of my body.

Jim shook his head. "I would have never forgiven myself if something had happened to you. After Kacey called the police, she let me know what was going on. You still gave us a pretty good scare, hiding out in that warming cabin. The least you could have done was put out some kind of signal."

I looked down, a little ashamed that we had made everyone worry, but it was worth every passion-filled minute we had spent alone. "We didn't have our phones, and Angelo left us out in the cold. We were lucky to find that place so close by."

"Well, I'm glad everything turned out okay, all things considered." Kacey took a step back. I didn't miss the little squeeze she gave to Rob's shoulder. Who could blame her? I don't know how I missed what a hunk Rob was all these years. His strong arms, well-sculpted body, his... well, I had a lot of catching up to do.

"It wasn't hard to run Angelo down in his McLaren either," Rob said. "Who drives a car like that in the wintertime anyway?"

I threw up my arms. "That's what I said."

Kacey flopped into the chair next to me and forced a smile, not quite masking her regret. "Too bad we had to lose that account. It would have been nice to have a win under my belt."

I grinned at her. "Don't worry about that. You're a fantastic coordinator. I'll make sure you have ten more where that came from."

Jim's eyebrows went up.

"What?" I said. "I always said hiring her was the right move. You should have done it a long time ago."

Now Kacey's eyebrows went up too. At this rate, everyone's eyebrows were going to be on the top of their heads.

"All right, maybe I wasn't as supportive as I should have been, but you really are great at this. I promise, we're going to be a great team."

"Team?" she hesitated. "Did I hear that right?"

I nodded and pulled out a folder tucked at my side. "In fact, here's your first official account."

She opened the file, and her eyes went wide.

"I met Frank Landin at the mixer the other night. He called me over the weekend and wants to set up several high-end events for his nonprofit this year. I told him you would give him a call."

Kacey shook her head. "But you ..."

I held up a hand to avert her objection. "He is all yours. Besides, I'm going to be a little busy over the next couple of weeks. I have a date with a good-looking Ranger and a 1954 Mercury Monterey convertible. Rob and I are going to take my Dad's old car up the west coast for a vacation."

I glanced over at Jim. "Unless you have any objections."

Jim shook his head. "You taking a vacation without me forcing you to? That's a bigger shock than Angelo's underground poaching ring."

I laughed. "I guess all this has taught me to appreciate life a little more. You're an amazing boss, a great friend, and I love my job. But there is more out there." I looked over at Rob and winked. "I think it's about time to dip my toes into the pool and see what it's like."

"Just don't wade in too far." Jim smiled. "I want you back."

"Don't worry, you can't get rid of me that easily." I grinned. Those few hours in the cabin had been the best moments of my life. Getting lost in that pool was exactly what I intended to do.

I hopped out of my chair to give Jim a hug. "Thank you for putting up with my craziness and not giving up on me."

Jim squeezed my shoulder. "I knew you'd come around, eventually."

I went to stand by Rob. "I need to wrap up a few things before I take off, but I know Kacey will keep everything in order while I'm gone. Don't miss me too much." I waved, then grabbed Rob's hand and whispered. "I have something for you. Let's go."

I guided him over to my desk in my cubicle, my nerves suddenly shifting into high gear, causing me to rethink my plan.

"What are we doing? Where are we going?"

"Shhh." I let out a nervous laugh. "Just be quiet a minute. I have something to ask you."

When we got to my desk, I put my bag down top of it.

Rob started whistling and looking around.

"Quiet," I said as I turned to rummage through my bag; my hand shook as I tried to find the small box. "You're ruining the moment."

"Wow, are you going to ask me to marry you?" He laughed.

I turned so fast at his comment that the item in my hand fell to the ground. I dropped down and scrambled to grab it. Looking up at him, I smiled. He was now dead silent, and the expression on his face was a combination of confusion and maybe even a little fear.

This was not playing out as I had planned, but there was no

turning back now. While still on my knees, I flipped open the little box, trying my best to steady my hand. "Will you move in with me?" I smiled.

He reached down, took the silver key out of the box, and grinned.

"This may seem sudden," I spewed out before he could answer. "But it's not like we don't know each other. It will make it easier while you sell your house and after our amazing evening at the cabin ..."

He pulled me to my feet and kissed me. The warmth of his lips and the tenderness of the moment made my legs want to buckle, but his strong arm held me steady.

"I'd love to be your roommate," he said when he pulled away again. "But we still meet at Grumpy's every day after work."

"I wouldn't have it any other way."

THANKS

Thanks for reading *Big Game*. If you enjoyed, it please leave a review on Amazon, Kobo, Goodreads, and/or iBooks. Reviews are greatly appreciated and will earn you a free virtual martini for your efforts.

Do you have questions, comments or ideas for future books?
Want to be part of the VIP Team?
Contact me: Ckwiles2@gmail.com
Follow me on Facebook and Twitter

www.ckwiles.com

Curtain Call Series

The Plaisir De Rouge theater, with its cast of quirky characters, is the backdrop for this hilarious and steamy romantic comedy series. Showtime Rendezvous, the first book in the series, is a steamy second chance romance where we meet Kristin and her long-lost love, Devon. In Stage Bound, Kristin's BFF, Fran finds herself tied-up, center stage in this blunder-filled workplace romance. Kristin and Devon then return to the spotlight in book three, Bared Secret, where a series of misunderstandings test their relationship, while uncovering a century old secret.

Showtime Rendezvous

Stage Bound

Bared Secret